DOWNHILL TO DEATH

'An accomplished first'—*Guardian*

When drama teacher Julia Feather calls a rehearsal of the Holmbrooke High School play on Sunday, everyone turns up—except Julia. That evening her body is found; she has been murdered. The town of Cloughton is stunned to discover it has a killer in its midst. But was Julia the victim of a random attack? As the murder investigation progresses, Detective Inspector Browne and Constable Jennie Taylor discover Julia led a far from innocent life.

DOWNHILL TO DEATH

DOWNHILL TO DEATH

by
Pauline Bell

Magna Large Print Books
Long Preston, North Yorkshire,
England.

British Library Cataloguing in Publication Data.

Bell, Pauline
    Downhill to death.

    A catalogue record for this book is
    available from the British Library

    ISBN 0-7505-0952-X

First published in Great Britain by Macmillan London Ltd.,
a division of Pan Macmillan Publishers Ltd., 1994

Magna Large Print is an imprint of
Library Magna Books Ltd.
Printed and bound in Great Britain by
T.J. Press (Padstow) Ltd., Cornwall, PL28 8RW.

0466225

For Viv

I acknowledge with thanks the help and information offered by Audrey Johnson and David Wilkinson, and, once again, by David Lord.

Prologue

Over the top of his copy of the *Cloughton Clarion*, Detective Constable Benedict Mitchell watched his wife as she came into the sitting room, her arms full of fleecy white towel and squirming red baby. She installed herself and son in the armchair opposite him and wrinkled her nose at the gas-fed, imitation live coals. 'I hate pseudo-cosiness but it's a bit chilly in the bathroom. I'll dry him in here.'

Mitchell decided to earn himself points by voluntarily folding his paper and making bright conversation. 'You can put up with it for another couple of months.' He jerked his head in the direction of his son. 'When he's a bit more mobile we'll have to think about leaving the flat and finding a house.' He regretted his suggestion as soon as it left his mouth and was relieved when she demurred.

'Let me get my exams over before we start house-hunting. We might be a lot worse off. There's no problem with the pram on the ground floor and we've got the use of the garden.' Virginia checked that the nappy was firmly in place, then reached for the bright yellow Baby-Gro suit and began to inveigle sturdy limbs into its extremities.

Mitchell hastened to agree. 'All right, we can manage for now. We'll move when his sister arrives.' The brief but caustic glance in his direction told him that this was the wrong thing to say too.

Hungry and cross, eight-month-old Declan noisily changed the subject for them and his father departed to the kitchen. He returned holding mashed vegetables in a plastic dish and hiding a bottle of warmed milk behind his back. 'Shall I feed him?'

Virgina shook her head. 'I've had lectures all afternoon so Mum's had him and I've an essay to finish tonight, I want to enjoy him now.' Mitchell beamed and reached for his paper again. 'Read it out to me,' Virginia instructed, expertly keeping frantic fingers out of the food with her elbow whilst she used both hands to tie on a bib. 'The ten o'clock news headlines keep me up with the national news but I'm getting out of touch with things locally.'

The infant beat a tattoo on the high

chair tray as his father regarded him dispassionately. He would grow into his handsome features but they were too strong just now for the soft infant contours they lived in and he was a hobgoblin. Thank goodness he hadn't been a daughter. People expected girls to be pretty.

For Virginia's benefit he turned back to page one. 'Bulldozers moved in on a derelict block of flats in Elizabeth Street, Cloughton, today, paving the way for a dream for fifteen would-be housebuilders. The flats have stood empty since Cloughton Council—' Declan renewed his screams.

'He's not interested,' Virginia remarked, phlegmatically. 'Neither am I! Try something else.' She began to shovel the brown mess into her son's mouth.

'Mason's, the chemists in the town precinct, suffered a break-in last night. The thieves entered by the kitchen window behind the shop which overlooks the lane between Mason's and Green's, the jewellers. Mr Jack Mason said that two heroin compounds with a street value of thousands of pounds had been left behind in the controlled drugs cabinet.' Mitchell looked up. 'Nice of the *Clarion* to advertise it. Richard Dean's dealing with that job.

11

He was saying there were some other funny features about it, but I didn't hang around when I came off shift to hear what they were. I'll hear more at tomorrow's briefing than they've got in the paper. What else do you want?'

'Isn't there anything about the charity walk?'

Mitchell scanned the pages. 'They're still appealing for last-minute volunteers. It's not very sensible for them to mention in the next paragraph that the forecast for the holiday weekend is unsettled with squally showers. That should decide all the ditherers to spend the night in their beds like sensible people.'

'Why do they have it through the night?'

Mitchell shrugged. 'Well, it suits us very well. It means there aren't many traffic problems. I think the real reason, though, is that it makes it more of an adventure for the kids who walk. And they're all quite safe. The event's always well organized with close on a hundred marshals.'

Virginia showed her son his empty dish and reached for his milk, testing its temperature and inserting the teat into a mouth that had opened to protest. When she looked up, she was not surprised that, the cricket season being just under way, her husband had reached the back page.

'There's nothing about this week's league games!' He was hotly indignant.

'So what is on the back page?'

Mitchell's tone expressed his disgust. 'Some kids' athletics meeting. "Holmbrooke High School, which opted out of council control in the New Year, has celebrated by carrying all before it at the first of the four district inter-schools' athletics meetings at Crossley Park." '

Virginia shrugged. 'It's that one out at Green Royd. They always had to be the biggest and the best at everything even when we were both at Heath Lees—you know, doing Shakespeare plays when we were only putting on one-acts, and so on. Though we were planning a performance of *The Winter's Tale* before you banged up Mr Frayn. Mum went to hear Holmbrooke's choir do Britten's *Ceremony of Carols* last December and they're doing something ambitious again in the summer. It's something new for them to shine in the sports department though. Heath Lees always beat them in our day.'

Virginia removed the teat from her son's

four clenched teeth, noted thankfully his drooping eyelids, and propped him on her shoulder. He burped in self-defence before the back-beating could begin. She beamed at Mitchell triumphantly. 'There you are. He's ready.'

Mitchell removed the supine bundle from his wife's shoulder and bore it towards the bedroom, pausing in the doorway and turning back to her. 'I'd better investigate this wonderful school. We might do worse than get his name down for it.'

Chapter 1

In spite of it being Bank Holiday Sunday afternoon, a rehearsal for Holmbrooke High School's current production should have been under way. Adrian Naylor, its assistant producer, had not minded turning out for it. The weather, with its usual cussedness, had deteriorated for the public holiday. The previous week's hot sun had produced a profusion of May blossom that today's spiteful rain-laden gusts were rapidly spoiling.

Throughout the weekend he had been unable to coax Fiona out of the house and an afternoon with the lively Julia, even in the additional company of a couple of dozen unruly pupils, would make a welcome break. They wouldn't be too boisterous, anyway, when Kit Travers arrived to see how they were all getting on.

He registered with approval, as he entered it, that an obliging caretaker had taken the edge off the unwelcoming chill of the school hall. It had been built and equipped at a time when education was considered sufficiently important by the town council and the inhabitants who elected it for them to put their hands deep into their pockets for its furnishings. The stage and window curtains were of thick velvet, though faded now and threadbare in places. Tall windows were ranged on both long walls and the narrow plastered strips between them were adorned with gilded honours boards. Only Oxford and Cambridge entrances were commemorated on them. They were not sullied by any mention of redbricks or polytechnics, which merited merely a reference on the back page of the school magazine and at the end of the list in the middle of speech-day programmes.

The beautifully polished parquet floor was marred this afternoon by evidence of recent sliding across it. The sliding had ceased momentarily, whilst a collection of youngsters turned to see who had arrived to supervise them. Reassured that it was only Mr Naylor, they recommenced their forbidden game and Adrian realized with a sinking heart that neither Julia nor Kit had yet arrived. Being on his own with the little monsters turned the deep stage and its commodious wings into a liability. It offered innumerable nooks and crannies where his cast could perpetrate all manner of evils. A muffled, mechanical squeaking confirmed his fears.

'Leave those curtains alone!' Stifled giggles greeted the nervously aggressive command and the two huge stage curtains continued to jerk spasmodically until they met. Safe behind them a well-developed youth with the beginnings of a beard grabbed a third-form girl.

'Hanging around me again, young Mandy? You must have known it was your lucky day.' He hemmed her in between the front flat and the enormous wheel he had just wound to activate the curtains.

Mandy was more scared than flattered. 'Don't, Michael, please don't.' She wriggled and squirmed to avoid him, but didn't dare cry out. Michael lowered his head and she whimpered softly as he began to nibble her ear. After some seconds he released it and offered her his own. 'Your turn, sweetheart.'

When his fingers bit into her arm, the child forced herself to take his left earlobe between her teeth and felt, without understanding, his wriggle of pleasure. 'That's nice.'

She shut her eyes in case the tears escaped and exacerbated the tormenting. How could it be nice? It was wet and nasty and since her front teeth were sharp it probably hurt him. She leaned against the metal wheel and prayed for a way to draw someone else's attention.

An intervention, divine or otherwise, released her. 'Pick on someone your own size, Mick. Let her go and play Ring-a-Roses with her little friends.'

Michael scowled but released his victim and she scuttled away. 'Keep your nose out of my business, Stevens, if you don't want favours withdrawn,' he muttered.

Daniel Stevens, hastening to change the subject, stuck his head between the curtains, then withdrew it. 'Typical!'

'What is?'

'That the person whose idea it was to spend a holiday afternoon penned up in school is the one we're all waiting for. There's only Wet Naylor here. He won't get anything organized.'

A smartly dressed blonde woman, who had slipped through the back door of the

18

hall, was making the same point, though more tactfully, to Mr Naylor. He was quick in Julia's defence. 'It's only part of an afternoon and she's only a few minutes late.'

'More like twenty. I'm not surprised the kids are playing up.'

'She's got a lot on just now. She's probably been held up with the charity walk arrangements.'

Miss Deakin was not placated. 'That's no excuse. If she thought she'd be too busy to get here on time then the rehearsal is even more of an imposition on us. She's got her finger in every flaming pie! Anyway, she's not busy with any duties. She's out having lunch with a friend.'

The curtains had parted a little way and the children had fallen silent to enjoy the public dispute. Realizing it, the needlework mistress lowered her voice. 'That was a bit unfair, I suppose. She's put a lot of zip into this production since she took over. I'm beginning to feel some enthusiasm for it myself. We'd better get this lot busy on something before they completely wreck the joint.'

Adrian saw thankfully that she was not going to leave him alone with the monsters, at least for the moment. They were still quiet, hoping for the small tiff to escalate, so, with Miss Deakin's borrowed authority, he got the rehearsal under way.

'We'll start with a re-run of the opening scene that Miss Feather laid out last time. Remember that this scene presents one section of a very complicated plot...'

The children's eyes glazed as they were reminded of what they had not forgotten. He knew they rarely forgot instructions from the charismatic Julia. As the characters in the scene made their desultory way to whichever side of the stage they needed to be, he willed her, for a score of reasons, to arrive quickly.

'I'll nip up to my room and unlock the costumes,' Hilary Deakin hissed in his ear. 'If Julia hasn't shown up by the time this scene's finished, we can at least have a trying-on session.' The hall door swung shut behind her and Adrian's heart sank as the news that she had gone was relayed to the wings and the giggling and scuffling broke out again.

'Be quiet this minute!' he roared, the panic in his voice delighting his tormentors. 'Darren Potter, if you can't behave yourself better than that the play can do without you. You're only a fairy.'

Wild guffaws greeted this reprimand so that the cast failed to register the arrival of Mrs Travers. The laughter stuttered to stony silence as, one by one, they noticed her. She glared at them. 'I should think so! Sit down.' They dropped cross-legged on to the stage as she turned to Adrian. 'Where's Julia?'

She watched him as he repeated his surmises and excuses. He looked no more than a schoolboy himself, though not of the same type as his persecutors. Resignedly, she realized she would have to take charge.

The third-form girl breathed a sigh of relief that her harassment was over for the afternoon. Even Michael wouldn't get on the wrong side of Mrs Travers. She smiled at Daniel Stevens who had rescued her and moved closer to him as they all listened to the head of English's instructions.

'I expect this scene to be fairly polished by now. Mrs Crossley worked on it with you before she left and Miss Feather went over it again last time.' She noticed and wondered about the significant glances they exchanged, but continued. 'Some of you older boys at least might have put the furniture on the stage. Now we'll have to

21

waste more time...'

Adrian Naylor and half a dozen children began to explain. She raised a hand to shut them up, then pointed to Michael.

He stood up, politely. 'Miss Feather said that having to walk round all that paraphernalia slowed down the opening. She said the human characters have to make their impact and explain their problems quickly. It was quite difficult acting with no props. Miss Feather said it was a challenge.'

Kit Travers frowned. 'The first night's only three weeks away. It's far too late in the day to make drastic changes like that. Put the scenery out as it was before.'

Michael's tone was courteous. 'Miss Feather said to take all the blocks back to the store, Mrs Travers, and it's locked now.'

She had her master key in her handbag but was running out of patience. 'Do it Miss Feather's way, then. At least it will help to fix your words.'

Helen Rowe, who played Helena, stood up beside Michael. 'We're all word-perfect now, Mrs Travers. Miss Feather won't work with us until we know our lines.'

Mrs Travers looked startled. 'You'd

better show me, then.' Another thought struck her. 'What are you doing here, anyway, Michael? And Wendy and all the juniors? We're working on Act One this afternoon.' She fended off another barrage of explanations and pointed this time to Helen, whose pretty face puckered as she tried to explain her concepts.

'Miss Feather put in a little mime as a prologue to the first scene—to show the role of the fairies. She said they're alien and dangerous and they manipulate the mortals all through the play without them knowing it. Puck has the closing lines in the last act so Miss Feather said it makes a framework if they appear at the beginning.'

'You mean she's added a scene of her own to a Shakespearian comedy?'

The girl seemed uncertain whether Mrs Travers' tone was incredulous or sarcastic. She glanced at Michael who smoothly took over. 'That was the reason, Mrs Travers, for taking away the scenery. The fairies do their mime and disappear into the wings. Then the first scene with the humans begins and the audience isn't sure whether they are seeing Oberon and all his minions in their forest home or whether they're actually hovering over Theseus and Hippolyta's state apartments.'

Mrs Travers' lips tightened: 'Let me explain what happens in Scene One.' The tone was grim. 'Egeus says Hermia must marry the suitor he's chosen for her. Hermia says she won't. The Duke says she must do as her father tells her or accept her punishment. She and her lover plan to elope. They foolishly reveal this plan to Hermia's friend. That's it! No Oberon, no Titania, no sprites, no hobgoblins!'

'And no fairies!' muttered a daring spirit. Mrs Travers' glare quelled the incipient giggles. Adrian Naylor bobbed up beside her and she became aware of the slight to him, implied by getting her information from the pupils. She glanced at him impatiently. There were eruptions on his cheeks where he had attacked the dark stubble. He had the sort of skin that was probably allergic to the various potions with which he had anointed it for Julia's benefit. Didn't he have a woman, though, living with him in his flat. Fiona, wasn't it? She was surprised he had captured one woman. He certainly wouldn't be able to cope with the conflicting demands of two. His jacket was an unflattering smooth serge in a hard shade of navy. He probably thought it smart. She looked at him again and decided he might look quite attractive in soft brownish tweeds and a casual sweater.

Taking in his glum expression and the highly indignant ones of all the junior fairies, she suddenly laughed. 'Forget all that. You can show me this intriguing innovation.' They leapt up with alacrity and, after a nod to begin, went into their routine.

In spite of herself, Mrs Travers was impressed by their mime, though she did not yet accept its validity. Julia had certainly inspired the cast with enthusiasm for her interpretation which made the little scene effective, and the conventional opening that followed was certainly much snappier than Mrs Crossley's version had been.

The Duke and his lady, showing a convincing and ardent impatience at the slow approach of their wedding day, were interrupted by the furious Egeus.

'Full of vexation come I, with complaint Against my child, my daughter Hermia—'

Mrs Travers was obliged to interrupt. 'Just a minute, Andrew. Where *is* your daughter Hermia?'

Michael, the source of all knowledge, volunteered, 'She's not here yet. She was supposed to be having a lift with Miss Feather.'

Mrs Travers controlled her mounting anger with difficulty. 'Has anyone rung either of them?' She glanced at Adrian. No, he wouldn't have. With exaggerated politeness she requested he make the calls and was pleased when the door that opened to let him out admitted Hilary Deakin, her arms full of costumes.

Mrs Travers' presence prevented the cast from milling round, so that Hilary, unimpeded, could drape a row of canvas chairs with elaborate cloaks, dresses and doublets. A gasp of admiration from Mrs Travers as well as the girls in the cast greeted the appearance of a long slinky tunic, composed entirely of overlapping silver-green leaves. Hilary held it up. 'This is for Titania. Take it to my room, Wendy, and try it on. Don't force the zip if it's tight.' Envious glances followed Wendy's departure. 'Still no Julia?' Hilary asked.

'No, and now we're without Emma too.

Julia was supposed to pick her up.'

'Why, for goodness' sake? It's no distance. Couldn't she have walked? And where's Julia got to?'

Mrs Travers shook her head. 'Don't ask me. I'm her cousin, not her keeper. Adrian's trying to ring them both—now that I've suggested it.'

Wendy reappeared, sinuous in her green leaves.

'Cor, roll on autumn!'

Mrs Travers' lips twitched at Daniel Stevens' quip and the cast felt free to laugh. Adrian reappeared to announce that Julia could not be raised. 'I've told Emma someone will pick her up to save time. Shall I go?'

Casting her eyes to the ceiling, Mrs Travers dispatched Adrian to the staff room to make coffee and handed Hilary her car keys. Twenty minutes later she had labelled each costume with its wearer's name and details of any alterations it required.

She looked up from her labours as Hilary re-entered, in her wake a dark-haired girl wearing frayed jeans, sunglasses and an air of trepidation.

'It's all right, Emma. It's not your fault

you're late. You've not had a message from Miss Feather? And for pity's sake take off those dark glasses. We're not doing one of those modern productions with Lysander and Demetrius rushing about on motor bikes and Hermia looking like a thoroughly emancipated Hollywood starlet.'

Puck, played by Michael's younger brother, made subdued revving up noises but was dealt with by his wiser classmates before Mrs Travers could take action. Correctly gauging her deteriorating mood, the Duke Theseus once more embarked on his opening speech and was interrupted again by Egeus, this time with his recalcitrant daughter in tow.

Mrs Travers was increasingly impressed. The production Mrs Crossley had abandoned had been stilted and awkward and Julia had done wonders. She let the scene run on, smiling as Helen, in her namesake's role, petulantly complained.

'For e'er Demetrius look'd on Hermia's eyne,
He hail'd down oaths that he was only mine.'

She leaned across and muttered in

28

Hilary's ear, 'Helen at least isn't typecast. If one of her admirers had really defected she would have dismissed him with searing contempt and allowed the next young man in the queue to take his turn. Julia's got her to withdraw herself completely and project only her character's fecklessness and petty spite.' The scene closed with a ripple of applause from the watching fairies and Mrs Travers glanced at her watch.

'If the rest of your production is as much improved as Scene One then I'm looking forward to seeing it. And now, if we're all spending the better part of the night pounding the streets, we'd better have an early tea and a few hours' sleep. We'll stop now. I congratulate you on what I've seen. It's splendid.'

Their pleasure at this hard-won praise was lost in astonishment which only the intrepid Michael voiced. 'Are you doing the charity walk, Mrs Travers?'

'I'll forgive your unflattering incredulity so long as you sponsor me.' She handed over her book for Michael to sign and there was general laughter.

Dismissed, the cast rushed outside, most climbing into the various cars awaiting them. Mrs Travers' face registered concern

29

as she regarded Hilary. 'Was Julia driving you back? I'll give you a lift then.' She filled the back seat with plastic carrier bags full of costumes to be altered and watched Hilary arrange her elegant legs around more of them at her feet. 'I can't believe Julia has just forgotten to turn up.'

Hilary shook her head. 'Of course not. She warned me not to be late when she left for church this morning. She was having lunch with a friend afterwards. Maybe the friend had an accident—or maybe Julia did. She could have telephoned, though having called a rehearsal that we were lumbered with, perhaps she didn't dare... Just a minute.'

Hilary scrambled out of the passenger seat, spilling yards of satin from its plastic wrapping. In a few seconds she returned, having extricated a grateful Mandy from a group of older pupils who were piling into Michael's car. 'It looks a bit squashed in there. As we've got a spare seat and we're running past Amanda's house, I thought she'd be more comfortable with us.

Mrs Travers noticed Mandy's obvious relief and obligingly signalled in the opposite direction to the one she had intended. For a mile and a half they discussed the weather and asked about the child's other weekend activities until she scrambled out at her gate with profuse thanks.

Hilary smiled grimly. 'Sorry about that. I just had the impression that she didn't want to go with them. That boy worries me.'

'Michael?'

She nodded. 'He's a strong character and talented, if lazy, but he's too streetwise to be in school. Amanda's in my form and he's been plaguing her for weeks. I'm not sure whether he just enjoys tormenting her or whether he has illegal designs. Either way, he wants watching.'

'Think the others will cope?'

Hilary laughed. 'Helen's a match for half a dozen Michaels. Anyway, having his younger brother tagging along should cramp his style a bit.'

'And Emma?'

'It might do Emma good if he gave her a bit of a whirl—in fact he may have taken his chance last night. Emma was telling me, when I fetched her, that her parents are away for the weekend. There was a party at her house last night.'

31

'Without their knowledge, I'll bet. I'm surprised they left her.'

'They didn't. She's officially staying with her godmother but the godmother is broader minded than they think. She told Emma to ring her if there was any trouble, then left them to it. Apparently they had rather a good time and were feeling a bit fragile even this afternoon. She may have needed those dark glasses you deprived her of.'

Mrs Travers turned into a row of substantial villas where her cousin and Hilary shared a house. 'Won't Mr Saxby notice the depleted state of his drinks cabinet?'

Hilary shook her head. 'They probably brought along their own liquor. Michael's family are quite well-to-do. They let him treat that car as his own and, anyway, he and Helen have Saturday jobs though Emma doesn't. Her parents make her do a round of music lessons and tennis coaching and then push her nose into her books to keep her ahead of everyone in her A-levels.'

Mrs Travers pulled up outside the end house. 'Sounds as though Emma will understand Hermia's problems then.

We've found Julia out in one piece of typecasting.'

They walked up the path and Hilary unlocked the door framed by two magnificent laburnums in full flower. The sun suddenly appeared through broken cloud and the golden fronds seemed to soak it up, embodying for them the holiday afternoon they had sacrificed. If Julia was to be forgiven, she had better be at death's door!

Chapter 2

Michael's Astra had been parked in the space usually reserved for the deputy headmaster's Volvo. Even Michael, Helen noted, had not dared to appropriate Mr Gregson's place. Michael opened the door with a flourish and handed in his female passengers with mock courtesy. Helen folded herself into the remaining third of the back seat and tried not to squash Emma in the middle. There was no way they could have made room for Mandy and she didn't think Michael had intended to drive off with her. She was just his current challenge to authority, though he probably anticipated that the remonstrations would come from Dan or herself rather than Miss Deakin.

Michael didn't really find Mandy attractive. He probably wasn't even intending one of his serious campaigns of harassment. He just couldn't ignore the over-developed bosom on a thirteen-year-old who was particularly immature.

Michael confirmed her surmise. 'Got old Deakin nicely wound up. Did she think I was desperate enough to seduce her precious infant?' He reversed in a spray of gravel and headed for the gates. 'Might think about it at that. Good pair of knockers.' Getting no response he changed the subject. 'Hope the Red Cross have got reinforcements for when poor old Travers collapses.'

'She's only in her thirties,' Emma pointed out. 'She should be able to manage it. Dan's going to run it!'

Michael's brother poked him between his shoulder blades. 'It's more than I've seen you do. You get out of breath washing the car—when you don't get me to do it for you.'

Helen glanced across at Paul. The two boys looked very alike, tall, lean, strong-featured and swarthily dark, but really they were quite different. She wasn't sure how to describe Michael. She just knew that Paul, amiable, uncomplicated, hard-working and unassuming, was not like him. 'Someone said Mr Naylor was walking as well,' she volunteered, in an attempt to keep the peace.

'Only part of the way.' They all, including Michael, turned to look at Daniel, and the car veered towards the centre of the road. Daniel hastened to explain. 'My dad's marshalling on the canal bank. Mr Naylor's girlfriend's been ill and can't walk far so she's just doing that flat stretch and he's walking it with her.'

'Wet Naylor's got a woman?' Even the charitable Paul seemed astonished.

'You know her, don't you, Helen?'

Unwilling to share the woman's problems in front of Michael, she flashed a warning glance. 'Vaguely. She's called Fiona Manley. She's an old girl, I think.'

'Old? She must be completely past it if she's prepared to go around with Wet Naylor.' Michael pressed his foot down harder on the accelerator and they all

35

tensed. Helen saw that Emma's knuckles were white and her face whiter. She looked as though she was going to pass out.

She took Emma's hand and leaned forward. 'Michael, either keep to the speed limit or stop and let Emma and me get out.'

'Scared?'

'Depends what you mean. I put more value on my plans for the future than on the cheap thrill of throwing it all away at eighty miles an hour.'

Michael slowed to fifty and Helen felt Emma's fingers slacken their grip on her own. She was sorry for Emma. Why couldn't Michael leave her alone? Though, having given her a dizzying social whirl for a few weeks, leaving her alone was precisely what he was doing. What she really wished was that Emma would forget about Michael. It had taken her sixteen years to realize that the human race was divided into two sexes. She might have rejoiced more in this discovery if her first encounter had been with a more considerate example of the other one.

'Quite right, Helen. More haste, less speed.' Michael's tone was sententious and he and Daniel exchanged knowing glances.

Whilst she was wondering about it, Michael drew up outside Daniel's house and he scrambled out. Paul took his place in the front seat and, as they moved off again, the two brothers began to speculate on the reasons for Miss Feather's non-appearance that afternoon, their suggestions alternately lewd and likely.

By the time the car dropped the girls at the corner where their respective roads intersected, they had facetiously decided that Miss Feather must be dead. 'Nothing else would have kept her from watching Mrs T's face while we were doing our new Scene One. After all, it is quite nifty.'

Suddenly, Helen liked Michael again. He was embarrassed at enjoying his success as Oberon, but as pleased with his contribution to the play as she was with her own. It amused her to be Helena. She had felt, on the first read-through, that no real girl could be so gullible or spineless or disloyal, but now she thought there were people like that. She and Emma stood waving till the car disappeared round the corner.

'Scene One went a treat, didn't it? La Trav can be a cow but she always admits if she's wrong and gives you credit when you do well,' Helen said. Emma's eyes sparked and she had a tinge of colour again. She was relieved. Emma, she thought, spent most of her life pretending to be someone else, the daughter her parents wanted her to be. Hermia's problems were a bit like Emma's own. Helen supposed it must be quite a let-down for her to come home to a house where no fairies rescued her with magic spells.

'Feeling better?' she asked.

Emma nodded. 'Thanks. I'm glad Miss Deakin fetched me. I was afraid I'd miss the practice and I daren't start to walk in case Miss Feather turned up and was furious because I hadn't waited for her. At least I got most of the tidying up finished whilst I was waiting.'

Helen was indignant. 'But we helped you last night. Hardly anyone went home until the house was presentable.'

'There's ordinary tidy and Mother's tidy, but it's all right now. The folks'll never know I didn't spend last night revising the Hundred Years' War and practising my violin.'

Helen grinned. 'When, actually, we were re-enacting the war, especially after midnight. Won't your father miss his liquor?'

Emma was unconcerned. 'We used whole bottles. He hardly ever checks what's in the cellar. It might force him to admit how much he drinks himself. He keeps a careful check on the levels of the current bottles, though, in case I've had a sip of sherry.'

'You're not going to start on it again tonight, are you? Not on your own?'

Emma laughed. 'My drink is water bright—for a while, anyway. And after tea I'll go and see Aunt Laura and tell her the house is still standing, so I won't be on my own.'

'You ought to be careful...'

'So should you. Did you see Michael ogling up your skirt when he handed you out of the car?'

Helen was neither alarmed nor flattered. 'We all know Michael. I haven't the slightest interest in him so I'm a challenge. That's how he treats all girls who aren't impressed by him and who aren't positively ugly. That's even how he treats Miss Feather.' She grinned. 'A little bird told me he's been giving her a good time but I don't think I believe it. He probably started

39

the rumour himself.'

Emma was not so sure. 'I wouldn't put much past him and Feather does ask for it, though I think it's unconscious. She doesn't really mean to.' Another thought occurred to her. 'Michael might be having a crack at you to prove he can win you away from Dan.'

Helen tossed her head. 'Then he'll be sadly disappointed.' She looked at her watch. 'Are you sure you can manage? If your place really is ship-shape, I ought to be getting back. We've a house full of lunchtime-till-bedtime visitors. I missed out on all the lunchtime washing up but I'm expected to do my share of entertaining them after rehearsal.'

She saluted, crossed the road and approached her gate. Before disappearing into the drive, she turned for a moment and looked back. Emma was staring over the low wall, beyond which the land fell away down towards the canal, alongside which, in the early morning, her friends would walk the last couple of miles of the annual charity walk.

The pastor at the Mill Street Tabernacle had been much struck by the aptness of his

Sunday morning sermon on the intended activities that night of a good number of Cloughton teenagers, including the sprinkling of them in his congregation. He had laboured, therefore, over a colourful poster version of his text which now adorned the Wayside Pulpit outside his pre-cast concrete mission church behind the station.

This extra 'opportunity for outreach' had left him less time than usual for the preparation of his 'Word', but his congregation agreed fervently that the sacrifice of ten minutes from the morning preaching was a small price to pay for the poster's impact on heathen passers-by.

One of these, the curate of St Peter and St Paul across the road, had smiled to himself as he paused in front of it. He imagined the effect of the painted text on the spirits of the footsore walkers who would pass it in the small hours. 'Follow the steps of the godly and stay on the right path, for only good men enjoy life to the full.'

Seeing his rival-for-souls perusing his text, the pastor hastened out to give full measure. 'It's a wonderful passage and so relevant to these young people, facing a long walk in the physical darkness tonight and a longer walk through the darkness of the sin of the world.' His eyes glazed as he fell into recitation mode. 'The adulteress has forgotten the covenant of her god. Her path runs downhill to death...'

The Reverend Paul Parrish stopped listening. For a few seconds he considered using the passage as a basis for his own sermon later in the day but he dismissed the idea. There wasn't time to make the changes and, anyway, most of his congregation averted their eyes from the displays outside the Tabernacle, so would be unaware of his gesture. Besides, the members of his own congregation, whether their journey that Spring Bank Holiday Sunday had been 'downhill to death' or up towards Heaven, would be tired from it. He knew that the grey heads that would range themselves in neat lines in front of him at Evensong would be reposing on their respective pillows an hour or more before the annual charity walk began.

At least one head that bowed before God and Paul Parrish that evening was not grey. Fiona Manley's hair was golden-brown and fell in energetic corkscrew curls almost to her shoulders. Her face was hidden but the curate knew that it was round and unblemished, adorned with a short, turned-up nose, full but unpainted lips and long lashed, neatly browed hazel eyes. Her limbs were slim and, even in May, already tanned, her waist trim and her curves, well, curvaceous.

Parrish found her a sensual delight and a spiritual trial and limited himself strictly to shaking her hand and wishing her the compliments of whatever season prevailed. It was from his wife, Kay, that the curate had learned his temptress lived with but was not married to the dark, awkward young man who waited outside for her each Sunday evening.

Kay had failed to ascertain the reason why she brought with her one of those suitcases with wheels at the corner that enabled them to be dragged behind their owners. She left it in the inner porch during the service, picking it up when she left. Kay surmised that she came back to Cloughton for weekends, travelling to her week's work in Leeds or Manchester on Sunday evenings. They had only facetious theories about why the case was not transported in her partner's car.

Several verses from the Song of Solomon passed through his mind as Fiona stood and sat and knelt. 'Tell me, O thou whom my soul loveth, where thou feedest, where thou makest thy flock to rest at noon: for why should I be as one that turneth aside by the flocks of thy companions?... Thy cheeks are comely with rows of jewels... Behold thou art fair, my love...thou hast doves' eyes within thy locks.' However he preached, as he had planned to, from the New Testament lesson.

To Fiona, it was immaterial whether the text was from the Gospels or the Koran. The only challenge she had set herself was to get safely through Evensong. She had given up on the morning Eucharist, unable any longer to cope with the dreaded walk down the carpeted centre aisle to the altar rail. At the evening service, she could settle herself safely into her pew and, with luck, she would 'last' till the end without making an undignified sudden exit.

She had little attention to spare for the proceedings that engaged her fellow worshippers as each wave of terror flowed in and ebbed away. Every one left her even more frightened of the next in case it should finally engulf her and she would...what?

Explode? Lose all control?

After parking her suitcase on wheels in the porch, she had lingered there, ostensibly absorbed in the week's notices, safe in the proximity of the solid stone wall. She had come to her pew only when the opening hymn was well started. Only two more verses to stand through. The congregation continued to stand as the set service began. 'We have come together as the family of God...' Fiona willed Paul Parrish to hurry through the opening lines.

'If we say we have no sin...' She breathed a sigh for the blessed relief of confession. She was grateful for the freedom not from the burden of sin but from the necessity to stand. She sank to her knees and gave thanks for the stout floorboards beneath the hassock, the firm pew on which she steadied her buttocks and the ledge for books on which she rested her forehead. She was safely surrounded by solid oak.

The Absolution was all to short and the congregation rose again to sing the psalm. Fiona registered that it had twenty-one verses, of which they were to sing just twelve. As they reached the Gloria she was fighting faintness and an indefinable sense of impending doom.

Then they were seated again as a portly lady made her way forward to read the Old Testament lesson. The congregation fidgeted, finding the passage from Isaiah unduly protracted, but for Fiona it was a chance to relax slightly and attempt to pay some attention to the proper purpose of her attendance.

'All nations before him are as nothing,' the reader intoned with considerable panache, 'and they are counted to him less than nothing.' Not a comforting thought. Fiona closed her eyes and tried to let the tension drain out of her. When she listened again, the message was more encouraging. 'Even the youths shall faint and be weary, and the young man shall utterly fall, but they that wait upon the Lord shall renew their strength... They shall walk and not faint.'

Paul Parrish smiled to himself. He had abandoned the gimmick of borrowing a text from his spiritual neighbour across the road and stuck dutifully to the Prayer Book table of psalms and readings for this Trinity Sunday, only to find the Almighty had supplied him there with scriptures equally relevant to Cloughton's charity walk.

The reader returned to her pew, conscious of the favour done to the prophet by her fluent rendering of his words, and Paul Parrish's undisciplined gaze was drawn again to Fiona Manley. She was mouthing the Magnificat from memory as she gripped the back of the pew in front of her with whitened knuckles.

He continued to watch her at intervals during the rest of the service, motivated now by no lasciviousness but a very proper concern. Was she ill, or was she going through some spiritual crisis? The Creed, in particular, seemed to upset her. She stood, white-faced, eyes closed, not reciting it, as though failing in her struggle to accept its tenets.

The aspect of the Creed which had actually dismayed Fiona was the fact that it occupied almost three-quarters of a page and represented the necessity to stand for an unbearable length of time. She tried distraction tactics, concentrating on a very clear enunciation of consonants. 'On the third day he rose again...'—with the Ds carefully separated, but it wasn't any use—'...with the Life everlasting. Amen.'

She slumped in the pew during the curate's brief remarks, wondering why she put herself through the mockery of church attendance. Maybe it represented a last link with the positive, motivated person she had used to be before she was assailed by this mystifying, terrifying, illogical affliction.

Only the mercifully short closing hymn to face now. Just the two verses, over almost before the panic had started. She stacked her service books neatly before turning for the reassuring sight of Adrian waiting for her in the doorway.

She felt guilty about the way she used Adrian. She remembered the night she had been introduced to him at a school function for its former pupils. She had found him neither exciting nor attractive, not someone on whom she was anxious to create a good impression and so, ever since, she had felt safe and unthreatened with him. She had rarely had an attack in his company and she found herself depending on him more and more.

She sat in his house all day whilst he was at school. Then, he did the shopping before coming home. Far from being grateful, she was worn out by her day-long terrors so he usually did the cooking too. She had refused to go on holiday with him, and often she could not even face the friends he invited to the house. Her anxiety would reach a crisis where she implored him to get rid of them but refused to let him explain why. She couldn't imagine why he put up with her bad temper, depression, hopelessness and bitterness.

Shaking her head, she braced herself, stood up and turned towards the door.

He wasn't there.

Her knees refused to support her and her hands felt huge, swollen and clumsy. She could hear the blood beating in her ears. She sank down on to the pew again and tried to reason with herself. He might just be reading the notices that she herself had looked at earlier, but she knew he wouldn't be. He knew how important it was to her to see him waiting for her.

She'd given him a horrendous holiday weekend, unable, for hours on end, even to get out of her chair and walk about the house. He had not complained but been his usual understanding self. Hoping he would realize her desperation she had begged him to stay with her this afternoon instead of taking his rehearsal. 'Julia can manage perfectly well without you. She does everything herself anyway.'

How far had she undermined his

confidence and stability with similar remarks during the past months. He'd left her abruptly when the time to set out for school came. This time even Adrian must have had enough. She felt the ridiculousness of her fear more acutely than anyone else. What was it that she was afraid of? She'd read about her condition and knew it was not uncommon, but when it was upon her she believed she was the only person in the world who felt as she did. She continued to sit, stultified as the church emptied.

'Are you all right?'

Somehow she found the self-control to turn and answer, 'Fine, thanks, Mr Parrish.' She bowed her head as though in further prayer, hot with shame. This affliction must stay a secret. She denied it even to herself in her happier moments. Without changing her position, she began to plan how she would get back to the house—if Adrian would let her in. The nearest way was across the park, but high wide spaces were quite impossible for her. She'd manage better going by the little streets and alleyways behind it.

Making this vaguest of plans had helped to calm her and she made her way up the aisle, touching the end of each pew as she passed it till she reached the porch and her suitcase. Ignored by the few stragglers still gossiping in the churchyard, she grasped the handle. As always, she was amazed how unquestioning people were in the face of even her oddest behaviour.

Suddenly, Adrian was charging up the church path towards her. Fiona uttered a prayer of thanks more fervent and sincere than any she had spoken in the service. Safely in his car, the doors and windows closed, she began to take in what he was saying.

'Apparently, Julia had promised to drop off two or three of the juniors on her way home. Hilary and Kit went off together and I couldn't abandon the poor mites. Sorry to keep you waiting. I was breaking the speed limit during the whole round trip.'

'But why wasn't Julia there? You said the revamped opening scene was being revealed to Mrs T this afternoon.' Now her fear had subsided, Fiona had made a firm resolution to take more interest in

Adrian's concerns. 'I'm sure you managed very well without Julia.'

Fiona herself certainly could. If she hadn't let Adrian talk her into singing at the hospice Easter concert, she'd only have been a distant acquaintance of the wretched woman. She really should make the effort, Adrian had urged, to give those poor folk what little pleasure they could still enjoy. The staff still remembered how impressed they'd been when Fiona had sung for them at Christmas.

The patients who had heard her then, of course, were now listening to angelic voices. In the end, she had run out of excuses and energy and agreed by default, expecting to be able to stand for the performance against the comforting bulk of the grand piano as she had done before.

This time, however, there had been a raised dais of portable blocks for the performers to stand on with the piano at its foot. She had trembled at the thought of walking on to it but had forced her shaking legs to mount the two steps. Then, a blinding sheet of terror had blown all common sense to the winds.

Julia had come up on to the platform to

assist her, realizing something was wrong. She had hissed into her ear and Julia had nodded, taken her arm and somehow got her through the song. She had gone the second mile, taking Fiona home with her afterwards, parking her car right up against the hospice building so that Fiona could walk in the shelter of it to the blessed, shut-in safety.

She had loved Julia that night, drunk coffee in her comfortingly tiny sitting room and poured out her problems. 'I can't even shop alone, and, when Adrian comes with me, I still rush as fast as it's possible. And it's difficult to believe that all the physical symptoms have anything to do with a mental problem.' Julia had nodded, shaken her head, prompted, encouraged her to tell the whole story.

'I don't expect you to understand it. I don't myself, but I'm so grateful that you at least seem to accept it.' Having put her troubles into words, her physical distress had decreased, then disappeared.

The next morning, Fiona had come to her senses. She had let someone else know about her humiliation, her fears, her panic. And worse, Julia had determined to help her. She had become someone to avoid, even to hate, slipping up beside her and jollying her along, arriving on a visit—'Just passing...'

She had begun a campaign, giving Fiona tiny chances to test herself, unwanted opportunities to beat her terrors, like sitting on the outside of the double seats in the bus, like walking across the open lawn whilst Julia smiled encouragement from the other side, as though Fiona were a toddler taking her first steps.

And, finally, a section of her bloody charity walk to attempt—from Adrian's house, along the canal bank to Julia's car, parked a hundred yards further on. Fiona had managed it once on a good day with no one else there. If there was no one there to witness her breakdown, it often didn't happen. Fiona knew that, on the night and in the company of all the other walkers, the distance she'd rashly agreed to might as well be a hundred miles.

Three times she had picked up the receiver, prepared to dial, then put it down again. She couldn't make the call. No one ever said no to Julia. It was too much trouble to get her to understand that she was being refused.

Chapter 3

By midnight the rain was steady but the majority of the walkers, high on the heady music to which they had danced since half past nine, were undismayed. The instrumental group that had stimulated and accompanied their gyrations played them out of the hall and into the shiny wet street. There, the youngsters sustained the melody with their own voices until, at the foot of the first steep hill, they needed all their breath for the ascent.

Daniel Stevens did not sing. One hour fifty-five minutes was the time he had set himself for the completion of the twenty miles. 'Something around two hours' was the estimated time he had intimated to the *Clarion* reporters and to the organizers who awaited the walkers' return to the YMCA building.

The reporters had been interested. The walk was not a popular assignment. Two or three photographs of a few weary youths, identical in their jeans and anoraks and scarves, to the first arrivals the previous year and all the years before that they could remember, was small reward for hanging around half the night in the cold. Daniel was something new. He was wearing running gear which always made a better picture and his estimated time was approximately half that of the previous record holder. Even a failure to achieve his boast could be worked up into a good story.

The charity walk committee had frowned on the scheme. For one thing, it meant they had to be ready much earlier than usual to receive the weary, halt and lame at their destination. Two hours was hardly time to get their heads down. Besides, no one else could keep up with Daniel. The walk was well marshalled and there was a substantial police presence, but, on his own, the boy was considerably more vulnerable than the rest of the participants in the event, both to villains who might harm him and to accidents that might befall him. But Daniel's attempt to run the course had won him popularity in the town and the organizer had hesitated to incur bad publicity by forbidding him to enter.

To Daniel, who had not yet reached the magic age of eighteen, when he would be eligible to enter races of any length he liked, this was the only way he could get his twenty-mile distance timed and attested.

Not the least anxious amongst the back-up team was Neil Stevens, marshalling his scheduled stretch of canal bank. However, his son had passed along the towpath at twenty-one minutes to two, moving easily and looking comfortable. The rest of the way lay through town streets, well lit and mercifully flat. He had stopped worrying and begun to look forward to boasting.

Meanwhile, he and his fellow marshal could each take a short nap. No walkers were likely to appear for more than an hour and, when they did, the procession would be well strung out at this point, eighteen miles into the enterprise and two miles from home. He opened the door of his Volvo and offered the spacious comfort of his back seat. 'Go on, Jack. I'll wake you up in half an hour.'

Stevens blew on his fingers, then paced up and down the path between the two limits of his sentry area. The scene was dark and bright alternately as he approached, passed and left behind the sodium lamps dotted along the canal bank. The shallow water was choppy and a gusty wind flung in his face the litter left by the previous weekend's strollers. The rain had almost stopped but occasional flurries of icy drops numbed his face.

After his allotted half hour, Stevens roused Jack by rapping on the car window. Both men climbed into the front seats and Stevens produced a flask of coffee from the floor and a miniature bottle of whisky from the glove compartment. Filling a couple of plastic cups with a mixture of the two liquids, he handed one over. 'Thought you'd be walking, Jack.'

Jack took a grateful gulp. 'Should have been but Jules insisted that this path by the canal needed three marshals. Don't see why. No one's going to drown in seven or eight inches.'

Stevens warmed his hands on his cup. 'It's deeper in parts and, if a bit of tomfoolery leads to a ducking, we'll be held responsible for the pneumonia cases.'

Jack snorted. 'Bloody marshals are more likely to succumb, standing about in this lot. It's even freezing in the car now. Lord knows what it'll be like out in that wind.' He peered morosely through the windscreen at the hostile scene. It was not unattractive. A foreground clump of privet had no flowers as yet but the upper surface of its leaves shone glossy black, their undersides rougher and greyish-brown in the sodium lights. Stevens switched on his headlights and the quartz crystals in the stone wall glistened whilst the choppy surface of the canal became a kaleidoscope of gold. 'Hang about. Here's somebody and you haven't had your kip yet.'

Stevens looked startled until he recognized the figures. 'These two didn't start from town. Julia told me about them. One's a teacher from Dan's school and the other's his girlfriend. She's a nutter or had a breakdown or something. They're just going from the edge of Green Royd estate to the canal bridge.'

'What for?'

Stevens shook his head and they both looked askance at the vagaries of teachers and their friends. They watched as the couple walked, arm in arm, for a short distance, then blinked as the woman suddenly broke away and ran towards a clump of bushes. Jack's eyebrows shot up into his hair. 'Well, we haven't much money but we do see life!'

A woman's voice rose hysterically.

'Do you think we should investigate?' said Stevens.

Jack beamed. 'I reckon so. That's what we're here for.'

They set off towards the bushes, heedless now of the wind in their faces, but, before the confrontation could take place, Adrian Naylor appeared and approached them along the path. 'My girlfriend's not well. She can't go on walking. Could you organize a lift for her?'

Jack got out his radio and spoke into it importantly, his resentment quite dissipated by the need for action.

'Can't you...? Naylor indicated the Volvo.

Stevens shook his head. 'Sorry it's our headquarters with food and water and first aid. There might be someone else in trouble before long. You can sit in the back, though, while you wait, if you like.' But, to their astonishment, Fiona refused absolutely to leave the shelter of the bushes and the three men stood awkwardly until a standby car arrived on the other side of the wall against which Fiona was cowering.

She walked, clinging to Adrian's arm

with one hand and trailing the other along the wall till she reached the gap that let them through to the road.

Jack shrugged. 'Well, she seems to have no objection to a Fiesta. Let's leave them to it.' They nodded to Naylor and strolled back to the Volvo.

'Women!' Jack gazed sadly at his less than lukewarm coffee, then jerked it away when Stevens offered to cheer it up with further lacing. 'Don't ruin it in cold coffee, man. Let's just finish the bottle.' They each took a nip and Jack returned to his complaint. 'Stupid creatures! This one rushes behind a bush for a bit of slap and tickle, then screams blue murder when she gets it. And other one, our dear Julia, has got us stuck here like a couple of mugs. Bet she's found herself a nice warm indoor job. I wanted to walk myself. It's the first time I've missed in twelve years. She'd better have a good excuse for not being here.'

He was obviously in a talkative mood. Stevens listened and gave up on his half hour's sleep. There wasn't time for it now anyway. 'I won it in eighty-five. Got my picture in the paper. The *Clarion* always does a big feature on the walk. They'll have Dan in on Tuesday.'

61

'He was in last Monday too.'

Jack nodded, fished out a block of chocolate and handed over half of it. 'Saw it. He did well.'

Stevens chewed meditatively. 'Yes, he's come on a lot this year. He's always been sporty, enjoyed his school games and so on, but this year he's got very competitive, even aggressive. He wants to win. The house has got nice and quiet so we're all for it. No time for ear-blasting pop because he's always out training. In fact, since the play practices started up again as well, we don't know we've got a son.'

'Won't it muck up his school work?'

Stevens considered. 'Well, we are watching it. He'll have to lay off all these extras next year when he's coming up to his exams.' He pointed. 'Here they come.'

The first of the walkers came towards them and the two men turned from each other to watch them pass by, offering cups of water and examining for signs of blisters, hypothermia or exhaustion. Stevens continued to think about his son. He was glad Daniel had a part in the school play and a place in its athletic team. His wife was in no state to cope with the energy of an adolescent son and his friends, yet he didn't want Janet's illness to blight Dan's schooldays more than it had to. Jack, too, must have been thinking of Janet. The last of a large group of youths disappeared, tired but determined, into the darkness beyond and he came across to ask, 'How come you and Dan are both out tonight?'

'Janet's at the hospice.'

Jack's tone changed. 'It's come to that, then?'

Stevens smiled. 'Not quite. She'll be home in a few days. She goes for what they call "respite care". Gives Dan a chance to have a few friends in and me to have a few drinks with my mates at the pub and both of us to give the place a good turn-out.' There had been much talk of cancelling the walk when the weather had turned so cold and wet, but he had unhesitatingly supported the committee's decision to go ahead. The hospice was to receive a third share of the projected eighteen thousand pounds the walk would raise.

The rest of the night was uneventful. Long periods of waiting in the dark were punctuated with binding up a slightly turned ankle—'Just in case'—protecting several blisters with strips of Elastoplast and dispensing emergency rations. 'Maybe walking beside the water makes the punters remember that they're thirsty,' Jack observed. Whatever the reason, Stevens had to pour the drinking water into the paper cups more and more sparingly to make it go round.

'A good number of folks seem to have stayed the course this year.' As Stevens spoke he watched his breath form clouds in front of him. 'I haven't managed to count accurately but they've been flocking past us.'

'Aye.' Jack nodded vigorously. 'And there's nought much to stop 'em from here on.' The two-mile road walk into the city was level where it did not run downhill.

Stevens was glad when Daniel appeared on the path unscathed. After a short rest and a hot drink he had walked the two miles back from headquarters, ostensibly to bring his father a fresh flask of coffee. Whilst appreciating his son's real motive, Stevens was still grateful. After some minutes Helen and two friends appeared and Daniel joined them to walk once more to the YMCA. There seemed no end to his physical staying power. Stevens hoped he would be able to match it emotionally later in the year. Helen was very mature and would be a comfort to him, though Stevens smiled to himself as he tried and failed to see her as a mother substitute.

Dan's voice carried back to him, commenting on the early completion time achieved by Dr and Mrs Travers. 'The old girl looked quite fresh and perky though they must have really shifted.'

He called to his son before the group was out of earshot. 'Any of you see Miss Feather on your travels?' They couldn't help but the question had supplied them with a subject for gleeful surmise to enliven the last stage on their long trek.

Those walkers who were hoping their efforts would be rewarded with the contemplation of a spectacular and beautiful sunrise were disappointed. The sky gradually became a lighter shade of black which developed into a leaden shade of grey before the rain began to fall again. After the clouds had emptied themselves a little, the horizon became a line where greyish green below met pearly grey above.

Stevens felt he'd been on the canal path for ever when the two official 'last walkers' came into view. When these last walkers had passed them they were free to go and he and Jack began to tidy away the paper cups and the rest of the debris. The two new arrivals scouted round the area of rough grass beside the path and Jack grinned as one of them peered suspiciously at the trampled grass between the bush and the wall where Fiona Manley had taken refuge.

Satisfied that the area contained no injured walker needing rescue, the two men saluted Stevens and Jack and moved on. After a couple of minutes they reappeared, hurrying towards the Volvo. Stevens let down his window. 'Lost something? By the way, you haven't seen anything of Julia Feather on your round-up, have you? She seems to have disappeared.'

The men continued to approach the car and spoke only when all four were face to face. 'Yes, we've just seen her.' The older man's tone was expressionless.

'Right.' The irrepressible Jack was half out of the car. 'She's going to get a piece of my mind.' The younger of the last walkers came out of his trance and shook his head.

'It's too late for that, Jack. She's along there above the path, downhill from the

Rocks, stiff as a board.'

The pit of Stevens' stomach stirred and he knew that Julia's stiffness would not be just the result of too much exercise. The elder of the two messengers was swallowing ominously. Stevens prepared himself, exchanged glances with Jack, who had manifestly understood the situation, and followed the two last walkers to where the body lay. For a few moments the four men stood, silently regarding it, awed and awkward in the face of the inevitability of death. Julia's body had no visible wounds, though its garments were wet and rather muddy and the fibres were snagged.

The four men had a whispered consultation. In spite of the extraordinary circumstances the remaining two miles of the course still had to be checked for anyone who had dropped out between marshalling points and needed assistance. Neil Stevens agreed to take charge of this unforeseen emergency and contact the police and ambulance services, knowing that Daniel, in Helen's company, was unlikely to miss him. The two last walkers resumed their duties, one plainly anxious to be out of the presence of death, the other reluctant to miss the excitement.

'Don't say a word to anybody you meet further on,' Stevens called after them, 'or there'll be a huge crowd coming to gawp.'

Jack grimaced. 'Jimmy had better stay put with young Peter or he'll save the *Clarion* the trouble of putting it on the front page.' He glanced at Stevens. 'Sure you can cope? Only the wife's likely watching the clock till I get back.' Stevens grinned. Jack's Betty would never let him hear the last of it if he deprived her of this chance to be the source of the dramatic news rather than hearing it from one of her gossiping friends. Even so, he was surprised at Jack.

'Don't you think you ought...' but he was talking to thin air and, after summoning help on his radio, he began his lonely wait.

The body was awkwardly bent and as immobile as Jimmy had described. Stevens looked again at the face that kept its own counsel and had nothing more to communicate to mere mortals. That was how Janet would look in not very many more months. A squad car, parking on the far side of the wall, interrupted his meditations. Cloughton was proud of this annual effort and the amount it raised for charity. The police assisting in the organization were reinforced by off-duty volunteers. It was not surprising that someone had arrived so quickly.

The driver was a uniformed constable whom Stevens recognized. He had last seen him in the YMCA building nine hours or so ago, in jeans and an apron. Ham sandwiches and hot coffee would await the walkers on their return and the constable had been busy buttering bread. Now, on duty, he escorted a plain clothes man, exceedingly tall and thin rather than lean. Stevens scrutinized him as he approached. The face was interesting but not handsome. The fairish hair suggested blue eyes but the appraising glance Stevens received as the officer came closer revealed amber brown and lively intelligence. The constable addressed the tall man as 'Sir', but Stevens thought his manner not sufficiently authoritative for him to be in charge of the case.

'Detective Sergeant Hunter.' Stevens acknowledged the introduction and shook the extended hand, then stood back without speaking to allow Hunter to view the body. Stevens looked too and realized that they were not seeing Julia as she had really been. She had expressed her personality in the thrust of her hips as she walked, and the pout of her lips and the twinkle in her eye as she persuaded people that her plans for them were in their own best interest. This corpse had Julia's blonde hair and blue eyes and was dressed in Julia's characteristic garments, sporty and expensive, but it wasn't Julia.

He answered Hunter's preliminary questions, feeling indignant when the irritation in the sergeant's voice imputed to him the blame for the dereliction of Peter, Jimmy and the hen-pecked Jack. 'You people would have had plenty to say if the last walkers hadn't done the rest of their final check of the course as arranged,' he retorted. 'And, anyway, Jack's a damned sight bigger than me.'

Hunter hastened to placate him. 'You're probably in need of breakfast and bed but I'd be grateful for a quick explanation of your own part in the night's activities and the discovery of the body.'

Mollified by Hunter's change of tone and the freshness of a morning that was doing atonement for the rain-lashed gusts of the night, Stevens gave his account of his vigil on the canal bank. 'One of us at least had to be here by about one-fifteen because of Daniel, but he didn't need any assistance. Jack joined me a bit later and then the crowds started coming.'

'Did anything unexpected happen?'

Stevens hesitated, then briefly described Fiona Manley's hysterical departure from the course.

'What was her problem?'

Stevens shrugged. 'No one's sure. A breakdown seems the favourite theory. I only know Mr Naylor as a teacher at my son's school and I've never met the girl before tonight. Julia knew her.'

Hunter nodded. 'Tell me about Julia.'

'She got herself on the charity walk committee.' Hunter noted the reflexive verb and its probable significance. 'She worked hard for it—worked up a lot of publicity at school apparently. There was a record entry this year and plenty of marshals. We usually only have two on this stretch, but she said she'd talked a number of fairly wild and boisterous youngsters into walking and a couple of weeks ago she persuaded Jack to became an extra marshal here instead of walking the course. He was annoyed when she didn't show up herself.'

'And surprised?'

'Yes. I wasn't too surprised, though, because she'd gone missing yesterday afternoon.' He passed on to Hunter his son's account of the play rehearsal. The constable blew on his fingers and scribbled in his book.

'What did you think had happened to her?'

Stevens looked at the body, then away again. 'Well not this, but something fairly drastic I suppose. She's usually relentlessly reliable.' Hunter smiled at the phrase. 'The kids had a variety of flippant expressions but none of their slander was very likely.'

'You knew her well?'

Stevens shrugged. 'Moderately well, through the walk committee and the athletics club that Dan and she belong to and through school. Not really personally though. She was an intense sort of girl.'

Another car had drawn up beyond the wall. Silhouetted against it as they made for the path, its three passengers were a comically contrasted trio, one tall and thin like Hunter, one shorter and beefy and, between them, a small slight man. Stevens knew, from the way his manner distanced him slightly from the others, that here was the man in charge.

The officers stood back to let the tall newcomer view the body. When he had pronounced it dead, their work could begin.

Chapter 4

Chief Inspector Browne chose to walk the short distance from the canal at Crossley Bridge to his office at the station near the centre of town. As always, he rejoiced in the eccentric character of the place, caused by the steep hills surrounding it that had cut Cloughton off from the big cities nearby—Leeds, Bradford and Manchester—and prevented its growing to a similar size. In the valley bottom, streets of old sets were flanked by long-established shops with Victorian façades. They led, from different directions, to a row of modern buildings alongside the bus station, concrete blocks, crowned above shop-level with rows of office windows. Between the blocks and rising from behind them, a hump of moorland like a monstrous outsize animal seemed trapped amongst the Lilliputian buildings.

Arriving to find his team waiting outside his office, he wondered if he had enjoyed it for too long and hastily began his briefing. For Jennie Taylor's sake he quickly described the scene he, Hunter and Mitchell had witnessed on the canal bank. With Stevens dismissed, their routine had swung into action so that by the time Superintendent Petty had arrived a posse of police constables were searching the scene and the path was sealed off with official orange tape. In bright sunshine, the corpse, its stiffened and bent limbs sticking out at awkward angles from the stretcher that bore it, was being carefully eased through the narrow gap in the wall towards the waiting van.

The Super had made his routine speech which began, 'I see you've made your usual efficient start...' and ending '...leave you to it with the utmost confidence.' Browne, who no longer either believed it or listened to it, had wandered over to Ledgard, the pathologist, to hear his preliminary remarks. There had been more of them on offer than usual and Browne passed them on to his team.

'There was a slit in the back of the girl's jacket and, as far as Ledgard could see, in the back of the girl too. There was practically no blood to be seen by the naked eye, so, presuming death to have been caused by the stab wound—which we can't yet, of course—it didn't happen in situ. Rigor seems fully established which means she had been dead at least twelve hours.'

'So she was killed at or before two yesterday afternoon.' Behind his back, Mitchell sarcastically applauded Hunter's feat of subtraction till he met Browne's eye.

'The walkers won't be sufficiently wide awake to talk to us yet awhile,' Browne went on, 'though Benny trekked on to the YMCA to mingle with them and pick up what he could before they all dispersed.' He turned to his son-in-law hopefully. 'Did you get anything?'

Mitchell shook his head. 'You said not to let on what had happened so I just pretended to be looking for her. The favourite theory was that she'd eloped with someone called Michael Cunningham, but I don't think it was offered seriously. He's apparently one of her sixth-formers. She taught at Holmbrooke High out at Green Royd.'

Browne nodded and turned to his sergeant. 'Have I missed out anything, Jerry?'

Hunter thought not. 'I thought it was interesting, the way Stevens talked about her.' Browne waited enquiringly. 'He said she was an "intense sort of girl" and that she was "relentlessly reliable" and that she "got herself" on to the charity walk committee. I had the impression that she worked very hard at minding other people's business. By the way, where's Richard?'

'Following up the break-in in the precinct, but we might have to pull him off it. The team's depleted already and murder takes precedence even over theft of drugs—though we'll have to wait for Dr Ledgard's confirmation that it is murder.' He chuckled. 'By the time Dr Stocks arrived this morning, Ledgard had already certified death and made a preliminary examination. He told our revered police surgeon that he couldn't have a lie-in on a Bank Holiday morning *and* collect his fee for a job a colleague had already done for him. Stocks wasn't amused. Benny,' turning his back to Mitchell, 'was anyone seen on the towpath who shouldn't have been there last night?'

Mitchell gave an exasperated sigh. 'I didn't find anyone familiar enough with all the officially registered walkers to recognize someone who wasn't.'

His tone had veered dangerously near to insolence and Jennie cut in to prevent further provocation. 'You look as though you had a rough night yourself, Benny.'

Mitchell recognized that she had rescued him from his father-in-law's displeasure and grinned. 'You can say that again. Why aren't infants born with teeth? They seem to come with all the rest of their vital equipment.'

'Try asking a breast-feeding mother,' Jennie retorted, then returned to the matter in hand. 'Where do we start, sir, while the walkers and marshals are sleeping it off? Her house, I suppose.'

Browne nodded. 'That's right. And her colleagues. I want to know all about her, who's written to her, what's in her diary and her dressing-table drawers and on her bookshelves.' The inevitable action sheets were on the desk and Browne hastily penned them. 'Jennie, you're the only woman available to me this morning. I want you to walk through her life, be her. We'll take our cues from you. Sit in her house among her possessions and get to know her.' Jennie nodded.

Mitchell, seemingly bent on irritating his Chief Inspector that morning, cut in. 'Stevens said she lived with another girl. She'll not be too pleased if we ride rough-shod over her.'

'Of course not.' Browne's acid glance shrivelled even the intrepid Mitchell a little. 'That's why I'm not sending you. I trust you to play it by ear, Jennie. I'm coming with you to have a preliminary look around, but I'm leaving the rest to you. Jerry, you get on to the charity walk committee members who haven't been up all night—if there are any. And, Benny, you get a list of the school staff and begin talking to those folk she was friendly with who worked there. We're all trying to put together the end of her life. Back here at two sharp for a very brief comparison of notes. I need to be with Dr Ledgard in the mortuary at half past. Anyone who feels underworked, remain behind.' The office cleared quickly.

Hilary Deakin made no trouble for Browne and Jennie Taylor. They parked outside her pleasant stone-built end-of-terrace house and Browne nodded his approval of the whole row. 'Not tarted up,' he observed. Jennie knew he meant that the stone, darkened over decades by smoke from currently redundant mills and factories, had not been sand-blasted. She too found the house attractive. Its bay window was free from the imitation leaded panes that spoiled its neighbours. Inside a low stone wall, the small front garden was hedged with a pretty and freely flowering pink shrub. A laburnum glowed yellow by the front door, not matching the hedge but, in flowers, it never seemed to matter.

'Woman's talk,' Browne hissed at her as he hammered at the door, then he stood back to study the woman who answered.

Hilary Deakin's thick blonde hair was almost straight and cut very short around features which took well to this severity. She had darkened her brows and maybe her lashes but the make-up was discreet and her general air striking. He thought her expressions of sorrow at the purpose of their visit, as she ushered them in, were probably sincere. Browne stood with his back to the room, apparently absorbed in the view of the back garden as Jennie began the kind of conversation her CI had demanded. He was indeed impressed by the magnificent display of azaleas and rhododendrons and by Jennie's easy manner as she engaged in the sort of chat she usually tried to avoid.

'We arranged to meet in Manchester,' Hilary was confiding. 'We have these days out from time to time and I never know whether it's going to be the zoo or an evening of grand opera—or both!'

'I knew, in that outfit, it would be a man,' said Jennie. Browne grinned. His WDC was really doing her stuff and he too had to admit that he had appreciated the beautiful cut of the white jacket and black skirt that emphasized the pleasing shape they encased. Jennie continued, 'I was wondering if it was...well, "home made" isn't the phrase for that jacket?' Hilary had obviously accepted the credit for it with a gesture. 'You're in the wrong job. You'd make a fortune in fashion.'

Afraid she might overdo things, Browne turned round. 'What time do you leave for your appointment, Miss Deakin?'

'Eleven. If I talk to you first I could

leave you here, looking over the house and through Julia's things, and you could post the keys.' She looked shamefaced. 'It's dreadful news, isn't it? And here we are talking about clothes.' She gave Jennie an accusing glance.

'Was Julia interested in clothes?' Jennie asked quickly.

Hilary considered. 'Not particularly, except these.' She walked out of the sitting room they were occupying, across the hall to the dining room, gesturing to them to follow her.

It was difficult to imagine what the room would normally look like. Round the walls, on plastic coat hangers suspended from the picture rail and covered in clear plastic sheaths for protection, were a dozen or more garments in jewel-coloured velvets and satins. The table had been pushed against the wall to make room for a rack which held what Browne thought was a collection of swimsuits. Jennie exclaimed and admired.

Hilary pointed to the rack. 'These are the fairies' costumes. They're mostly the gym club members and Julia's got them—had them—doing extraordinary feats up and around the bars disguised as forest branches.

We've got to disguise the leotards too but there must be nothing floating or sticking out to catch their limbs in—and nothing too flowery either, otherwise all the boys will want to opt out. Jules and I were going to have a confab about it after rehearsal yesterday.'

'It sounds an interesting production.'

Hilary's fact lit up. 'It is now. The woman who was doing it last term got pregnant and was having a rough time—well, was making heavy weather of it, anyway, so she quit teaching and the play and took maternity leave early. It wasn't much of a production under Mrs Crossley. She'd cast it from amongst all the biddable children because her discipline was weak, to put it kindly. Julia came on supply to teach her lessons. She discovered the play had been abandoned and took it up again.'

'The cast hadn't lost interest then and forgotten their lines?'

Hilary grinned. 'The good ones hadn't and the others weren't interested in the first place—the girl playing Titania, for instance. She was a very pretty girl but a naff actress. Most of her lines had been cut out because she couldn't learn them.

Julia replaced her with Wendy Malik. She's a beefy half-caste girl who is wonderful on the stage, though a liability in the classroom.'

'The first girl didn't mind?'

'She was thankful to opt out. A lot of staff thought Wendy not the right type at all. They're going to get a shock—if we can keep going without Jules.'

'And can you?'

She squared her shoulders. 'We'll have to. We can't let the kids down a second time. But it won't be easy. They think of it less as Shakespeare's play than as Jules' production.'

'You could put it to them as a tribute to her.'

'There's an assistant producer, isn't there?' Browne put in.

Hilary looked puzzled for a minute, then laughed. 'Adrian Naylor, you mean? He won't take over, he's just a liability. He volunteered himself because he had a crush on Jules and he's got in the way all through. He's useless with the kids and devoid of all common sense.' She made another dart for the door. 'Come in the kitchen and we'll have some coffee. Do you know he found nothing wrong with offering to drive round and fetch Emma Saxby to rehearsal.' They followed her voice up the hall and took chairs at the kitchen table. 'He was quite oblivious of what the suspicious world would accuse him of getting up to with her.'

'Is Emma that sort of girl?'

'Heavens, no.' She banged the filled kettle down and switched it on. 'But teachers are witch-hunted for every conceivable sin they can't prove they haven't committed. Could you pass the milk out of the fridge behind you?'

Jennie obliged. 'What is Emma like?'

Hilary gave the matter serious consideration. 'An over-disciplined late developer,' she volunteered after a minute. 'Lately she's become very attractive physically, partly because she's developed a nice little figure and partly because she's got a huge crush on Oberon and has started making the best of herself.

As she dispensed the coffee Browne took over from Jennie and became more formal. 'Can we get on to this weekend now? Did Julia live here permanently?'

'No, but she didn't live anywhere else. She was brought up by her grandmother who died three years ago while Jules was at college. I told you she was on supply for Mrs Crossley's maternity leave. Mrs Travers is head of English and Julia's her cousin. I'm friendly with Kit, so I offered Jules a place here for the duration. It helps with the mortgage.'

'Didn't you see rather too much of each other, living and also working in the same building?'

She saw all the implications of the question and answered frostily, 'Once the play was re-started it was very useful.'

'And when did you last see her?'

There was an edge to Hilary's voice. 'It depends what you mean. I actually saw her last thing Saturday night, but we called out to each other yesterday morning. She was flying round the house getting ready for church and, it being Sunday and a Bank Holiday, I was enjoying a lie-in. I had lunch out yesterday too and left before Julia returned. It was with a college friend.' She reached into a kitchen unit drawer, took out paper and pencil and scribbled. 'That's the name and address. I went out before Julia came back. Sam gave me a lift to school afterwards and Julia was to have driven us both back for tea and a summit conference about those leotards.'

'Your car in dock, then?'

She shook her head. 'I don't have one. I prefer putting my money into property. It doesn't lose its value so quickly.'

Browne had been abrasive. Jenny was ingratiating. 'You must have been annoyed when she let you down.'

'Not really. She rarely does, so I was puzzled, worried even. What annoys you about Julia is that she thinks, if she does fail you in some way, that you wouldn't be able to manage. She treats you like a capable mother treats a retarded child—she used to, I mean.' She stacked cups on a tray and began restoring the kitchen to its former pristine tidiness. When she carried the dishes to the sink Jennie took a tea cloth.

Browne addressed Hilary's back view. 'What was Julia interested in besides school?'

Hilary sniffed and attacked a milk jug with the dish mop. 'Everything. She couldn't keep her nose out of anything. Whoever stuck a knife in her saved her from dying of exhaustion.' Jennie's indrawn breath brought a shamefaced grin. 'I didn't mean to be callous. I'm just telling you what she was like. There was teaching and the play and the athletics club. She's a fitness freak—runs, swims, plays squash. She's got a sort of boyfriend there.'

'Sort of?'

'Well, a man who's a friend that she liked working out with. It wasn't exactly whirlwind passion, though.'

'Any other men?' When she shook her head, Browne got up from the table. 'May we have a look round Julia's room?'

Hilary led the way upstairs. Jennie, setting off after them, noticed Browne's slight shake of the head. She dropped back and waited for Hilary to return to the kitchen.'

'One of the other constables,' she began as Hilary started to put the cups away, 'heard some youngsters gossiping about a relationship between Julia and a sixth-form boy. Could there have been any truth in it?'

Jennie received a long hard stare. 'Yes and no. In some ways Jules was just as much an innocent as Adrian. I suppose you're talking about Michael Cunningham. He's an odd boy, restless and unfocused. He certainly made a sort of play for her and Julia was usually pleasant to him when he hung around—and of course he was in favour for being a magnificent Oberon. He doesn't seem capable of the light-hearted encounters the others have with each other so he proves his prowess in other ways, like making a nuisance of himself with a girl in my form. She's only fourteen, physically well endowed but sexually quite unawakened. And then he had a crack at Emma.'

'She's his own age, isn't she?'

Hilary consulted her watch and reached for her handbag. 'I shall have to go in a minute. Emma's rather a mummy's girl. Girlfriends are encouraged but boyfriends might lead her astray from her Oxbridge ambitions.'

'Hers or her parents?'

Hilary smiled. 'Precisely. Anyway, the other boys keep off. Michael decided to show her a good time. When he'd got her interested he was satisfied and dropped her again. It probably did her good. At least she knows what she's missing now.' She took another glance at her watch. 'I'll miss my train if I don't go now. I'll be back at about midnight if you need me.' She placed a key on the table and departed.

As she reached the gate, Jennie had a sudden inspiration and called after her.

'Why don't you just splash those leotards with luminous paint? It would catch the stage lights and save an awful lot of sewing.' Hilary Deakin blew kisses to her as she ran down the road.

Chapter 5

If Browne wanted him to talk to the staff of Holmbrooke High, he would start at the top, Mitchell decided. The headmaster lived, as the DC had expected, in the upper middle class area to the south of Cloughton and the particular house in its quarter-acre of garden was just what he had anticipated. It was a newish, biggish, dressed-stone bungalow with lawns that were unmistakably the work of a professional gardener. A Rover and a small VW were parked in the drive and Mitchell found George Gregson entertaining his head of PE.

'Not knowing what had happened, we spent our holiday morning on a round of golf and only heard about Julia from the shower-room gossip. We're both quite devastated.' They didn't look it, Mitchell decided. The games man still wore sports gear but the headmaster was back in suit, shirt and tie. The DC parried their questions, refused the very dry sherry he was offered and accepted their willingness to co-operate 'in every possible way—not that I know much about her except what she did in school'.

Mitchell took the armchair Gregson indicated to him. 'Was this Miss Feather's first post?'

Gregson was busy refilling their two glasses. 'According to her CV she's been out of college nearly three years doing a series of short-contract jobs. No permanent position has materialized but she's never been out of work—which is something at least in these bad times.'

Mitchell cast a baleful glance at the games master who was keeping a low profile and making short work of his second sherry. He addressed his question to both of them. 'How did she fit in at Holmbrooke?'

Gregson paused to consider. 'She was invaluable to us in the short term. She took over Mrs Crossley's exam work, which was all we'd asked of her, but she was full of ideas. She started a sixth-form book review society and gave them a new slant on all kinds of writers. She was sporty and willing to help with games. She reorganized hockey practices so that the First Eleven defence and the Second Eleven attack played against the rest, a simple idea but new to us.' He leaned back expansively. 'She had unfailing energy for the school production and some very good ideas...'

The games master was suddenly moved to join in the conversation. 'She talked all the best gymnasts into being attendants of the fairy king and queen—in fact she involved just about the whole school in her play in one way or another.'

'All for her own glorification?'

Both teachers gave the question serious consideration before Gregson answered. 'Some people thought so. The discriminating think not. She was just alive with it...' He realized the inappropriateness of his his phrase and hurried on. 'It's the best Shakespeare production I've ever seen at school level.'

'Why did she not have a permanent job if she was so talented?'

Thinking out the best answer to this necessitated another filling of their glasses.

'Because,' Gregson said slowly, 'in an establishment which functions through its rules and regulations and routine, she was trouble. She had to make things happen but she hadn't much staying power. She disturbed and needled her classes, made them think things out, but she didn't keep them working steadily. When she left and Mrs Crossley came back, we'd have sighed and said thank goodness. A lot of her innovations, with refinements and adaptations, will be kept if we've any sense—but she'd have cancelled them herself if she'd stayed. She was too restless to keep anything the same for long. She was best as a sort of consultant, always needing a fresh challenge.'

Mitchell turned to the games master. 'Did she have anything to do with the successes that were splashed all over the back page of the *Clarion* last week?'

He shrugged and shook his head. 'I just don't know. We've not only reached a new standard of achievement in athletics, we've developed a whole new attitude to it throughout the school. Julia's played her part. I'd like to take some credit myself, but I haven't done anything recently that's different from usual.'

'It's the culmination of several years' hard work on your part,' put in Gregson, regarding his subordinate through the rosy glow of three sherries and whatever he had consumed at the golf club, but the PE man persisted in his modesty.

'I think Daniel Stevens' success has infected the others. He's always been a very popular boy and something of a leader.'

'But not always such a winner, I gather.'

Gregson looked slightly puzzled. 'Yes, that's true. He's always been well co-ordinated and a good runner, but his motivation and endurance are on a new level. It's partly that he's maturer, I suppose—and his home circumstances may have something to do with it. His mother's dying of cancer and his father, naturally, is very taken up with all the related problems, though he does his best for the boy. Daniel wants to make his mark—and possibly to exorcize his own grief in sporting excellence. Still, you wanted to know about Julia. You really ought to talk to some of the fifth- and sixth-form pupils. She spent more time with them than in the staff room—or anywhere else.'

With no evidence that he could show

to anyone, Mitchell was sure that Gregson had made advances to Julia and had been rejected.

Councillor James Bentley had been greatly annoyed by the discovery of a body on the route of the twenty-ninth annual Cloughton charity walk. He talked about it, Hunter observed, as though it were an act of metropolitan sabotage for which neither he nor his fellow committee members could take any responsibility. He enlarged on the event's trouble-free history.

'It's traditional for the walk to be organized by the editor of the local paper and a minister or representative from each of the four main churches in the town. The original editor twenty-nine years ago was brother of the canon at St Peter and St Paul. As you know, the paper runs a ballot in the early spring and the readers vote for the year's good causes. There's no registration fee, no charge for food. We send out sponsor books and every penny goes to the chosen charities.

'We prepare for every eventuality. The St John's Ambulance people are at the YMCA and each of the rest centres, on call all night. And there are at least one

when the walkers set off?'

Bentley shrugged. 'Well, you've caught me there. Julia wasn't, was she? But, in theory, there's radio contact. The course is divided into three sections. The leader in charge of each checks that everyone in his area is in situ. Since two men were on the canal stretch anyway, I don't suppose they worried. When everyone's left there's a team of clerks to check the sponsor books they've handed in to see what each walker owes. Then they've a rough idea of the expected total.'

'Which is?'

'It's a bumper year. The books promise almost eighteen thousand pounds. We always have a few bad debts but most of it comes in—quite a lot of it on the night, actually. You know how you usually pay up on the spot if some kid asks to be sponsored for something, then you don't have to bother remembering it. They bring it along and hand it in to anyone wearing a helper's yellow armband. All the helpers have to be insured, but they're told, if anyone approaches and threatens them, to drop the money and run.'

It had not previously occurred to Hunter that robbery might have been a motive for

Julia's death. 'Would Miss Feather have obeyed an order to abandon the loot?'

Bentley smiled. 'She'd be more likely to fell the robber with a lecture on depriving the needy and losing his own personal integrity!'

Anxious not to be late for the post mortem, Browne conducted his two o'clock briefing briskly. 'I'm assuming we're dealing with murder,' he told his assembled team. 'At least, we've never before investigated an accidental stabbing in the back. The victim was left an orphan at seven. She was brought up by a grandmother who died three years ago whilst she, Julia, was at college. Her nearest relative is a cousin, Katherine Travers, who teaches English at Holmbrooke. The body was found about twenty feet off the canal path, at a point below the Rocks. That's the local name for the escarpment overlooking the valley on the north side. It isn't actually rocky on the surface, except at the very top. It's just a very steep slope covered in rough grass and the odd shrub. Two of us had a look round Julia's house this morning.' He turned to his WDC. 'You did well with Hilary Deakin, Jennie.'

'That means,' cut in the irrepressible Mitchell, 'that she got all the information you wanted from tea-party conversation with no questions asked.'

'Got it in one.' Jennie grinned, and Browne nodded to her to summarize their conversation. 'When the CI had gone to look at Julia's room, Miss Deakin gave me a photograph.' Jennie produced it and passed it round. She had studied it herself as she ate her sandwiches in the canteen. Julia's attention was fixed on the photographer. She wore strange garments, a long clinging tunic and cropped trousers. Her hair was as short and blonde as Hilary's but quite straight with a piece on the crown left long and growing forward so that at one side it must have obscured her vision. Jennie could imagine the provocative gesture with which she would have continually tossed it back. She had all the marks of a poseuse, yet there was a frankness in her gaze and stance that suggested any provocation was not deliberate.

Browne was enumerating their morning's findings. 'Her purse contained a film chit. I've sent a PC to collect the pictures. Let's hope they're interesting. There was also a Cloughton Couriers membership card. In the wardrobe... Well, that's your department, Jennie.'

She described to the team the trendy tracksuits with their stripes and patches of primary colours. 'There was nothing very sophisticated except one black dress. The usual jeans and shirts were there and some knitted cotton garments. I wondered why she hung her pyjamas in the wardrobe until I looked closely at the photograph and saw that that's what she wore for lazing in the garden. There wasn't much that she might have worn at a party or a disco and very little that looked formal enough for school.'

'Her diary,' Browne continued, 'might be interesting if we had an interpreter. It's full of jotted initials and times, not an outpouring of her thoughts and feelings. No letters in the handbag or the room.'

'Hilary said she didn't write. Julia was an inveterate telephoner. She had a grumble about it. They split the bill fifty-fifty but nearly all the calls were Julia's. Hilary switched to an itemized bill to prove it. I asked her for it.' Browne beamed his approval. 'I got her to mark her own calls so we can check who Julia rang—from home anyway.'

Browne reached into his pocket and exchanged conspiratorial smiles with Jennie. He took out a cassette tape and placed it in the machine on his desk. 'Miss Deakin told us we had complete freedom to examine her house and possessions, so we borrowed the tape from their answering machine. I recorded two messages from it before I put it back.' He switched it on.

Even after Browne's build up, the team was not disappointed.

'Don't contact me again, Julia—at least, not on the same subject. The appointment's been made and will be kept. If you interfere any more, I shall have to take official action to stop you.'

After a few clicks and hisses, the messages continued. 'Namaste, Julia. Kyaa haal hai? Mai Thiik huu...' A soft voice continued the seeming gibberish. Without a clue to the meaning, Browne felt that the speaker was enunciating unnaturally slowly and precisely.

'Well, it's not French.'

'Well done, Benny. Anyone improve on that?'

'Not German,' Hunter offered, 'nor Italian, nor Spanish.'

'You speak all those?'

101

Hunter shrugged modestly. 'Only holiday phrases but enough to be sure that none of them is what we were listening to.'

'It isn't Swedish,' added Jennie.

Browne was amazed at this erudition hitherto unsuspected in his team. Mitchell, who felt he had given the least good account of himself, changed the subject. 'Do we know who left the first message?' Browne shook his head. 'So we ask Hilary Deakin?'

'Probably, if we need to. Funny to leave a message and no name.'

'No it's not. It just means they often spoke together. When I phone Ginny, I don't usually tell her it's me. She knows it is.'

Browne allowed Mitchell this point. 'There was a message from Neil Stevens but he did identify himself. He said he had a small problem and asked Julia to get in touch with him. Said he didn't like to bother her but he knew she'd meant it when she offered to help in any way she could.'

'What with?'

'We shall have to see. Any general comments?'

'The first speaker says "official steps".

That sounds like something legal, not as though he was contemplating violence. Interesting, all the same.'

'Hilary Deakin didn't seem devastated by the loss of her colleague. She made the expected noises but I didn't feel any need to commiserate with her.'

'True, Jennie. Jerry?'

'I was wondering how a needlework teacher comes to know so much about Michael Cunningham. Presumably he doesn't do A-level embroidery.'

'Interesting, though I'm not sure it's relevant.'

'And how,' demanded Mitchell, 'does Hilary Deakin know that Julia Feather was killed with a knife? I know it's got about that she's dead and there's been enough police interest to make people suspect foul play, but Jerry saw the body close up and he didn't realize she'd been stabbed till after Dr Ledgard had examined her.'

'Right.' Browne produced yet another sheaf of action sheets. 'We'd better try to answer our own questions. By the way, what did you get out of George Gregson, Benny?'

Mitchell scowled. 'Posturing prat! Stood there with his arm resting on the mantlepiece like a male model in a mail-order catalogue trying to make an eighty-quid suit look like Savile Row.'

Hunter grinned. 'You took to him, then?'

Mitchell repeated the gist of what Gregson had said. 'Which of them shall I see next?'

Browne looked up from his form-filling. 'The ones involved in the play, but I think we'll take Mr Gregson's advice and talk to some of these children. Jerry, you can start with the nicely brought up Emma and her parents—find out why Julia was picking her up when she lived so near school.'

'Good choice. Jerry's just the class of gent they'll like to talk to.'

Browne glared at Mitchell and his tone was steely. 'Travers family for you. Get off NOW!' Nonchalantly, Mitchell picked up his form and sauntered to the door. 'Jennie, try to hold on to your sanity whilst you talk to the love-sick Naylor and the highly volatile Miss Manley. I'm off to the PM. Then, if there's any afternoon left, I shall go to church, the Sacred Heart to be precise. Julia was last heard of preparing to go there. I'd better find out whether she arrived.'

Chapter 6

Emma Saxby hung the washing-up cloth on its hook as her mother, tight-lipped, put away the unused place setting meant for her father. For once she did not blame her father for not coming home.

She remembered her mother's words at breakfast. She was the grateful possessor of what she considered the aural equivalent of a photographic memory. Learning Hermia's lines had been effortless. She could recite the whole play now, more or less, though the easy flow of it would leave her when she was no longer hearing it so often. Her mother's words came back to her almost verbatim, maybe because they too were often repeated.

'You always talk about my nagging tongue, as though, because you haven't spoken any words, you haven't hurt me... You come down morning after morning and sit in an almost tangible blanket of ill humour... We all know that any attempt to communicate will provoke an angry attack and door slamming, but you pretend to yourself that because you haven't actually verbalized your displeasure, you haven't attacked me.

'You can look back in bitterness and say, "You said..." I can look back with equal bitterness and say, "You didn't say anything." Your disappointment, resentment, anger were just as clearly communicated.' It was that, or something very like it.'

Very fine words, Emma thought, if her mother's tone had not belied them. She was articulate, certainly. If only she dared to shock Father by losing her temper. Father only understood shouting, though he rarely shouted himself. Reason or sarcasm in Mother's nasal whine had no effect except to infuriate him.

Emma suspected that he had married her mother for her unmistakably upper class vowels but the complaining tone was all he noticed now, and he'd never listened to what she—or anybody—actually said. Emma looked around for her library book and tried to calculate what percentage of her time she spent hidden, within earshot of her parents' incessant unresolved arguments. At least, she consoled herself, she kept track of what they were plotting and planning for her so that she had time to prepare some excuses.

The doorbell rang and, looking into the hall, she saw her mother admitting an extremely tall, fair-haired man. As he was explaining the purpose of his visit, her father's car appeared at the door. Emma darted along the hall to the dining room, not hearing the details of her father's curt excuse for missing the family meal but catching the reply: 'Don't give it another thought. It won't matter to Sergeant Hunter that you spent your lunchtime in the Fleece.' Her mother turned to the visitor with her hostess's smile. 'My husband drinks most of his lunches there.'

Emma watched the policeman blink before he broke the news of Julia Feather's death to her and her parents. She knew he was watching them carefully. Emma remained silent. Her parents both managed conventional expressions of regret before reverting to type. 'That's it! Emma will have to change schools. We can't have her mixed up in this sort of thing. I always thought she was wasting her ability there anyway.'

Emma bit back a desire to giggle as her mother thanked the officer profusely for bringing them the news, as though the chief purpose of his visit was to avert any inconvenience that ignorance of it might cause them. She looked away from her mother, staring at the wall and saying nothing. Belatedly, her father invited the policeman to be seated, probably quickly regretting it when the sergeant asked them both for an account of how they had spent their Saturday.

'I hope you're not suggesting this unfortunate occurrence has anything to do with us.' Frostily, he explained his business commitments over the weekend, in some detail, and, Emma suspected, with considerable aggrandizement of the part he'd played himself. He offered his hotel receipt as confirmation. 'I presume this is sufficient evidence without any need to upset my wife or embarrass my business associates.'

The policeman was urbane. 'It hasn't come to that yet, sir. It may.'

'There's not much I could say to help you, Sergeant, upset or not,' said Emma's mother. 'Wives are not made welcome at the drinking sessions that seem necessary between business meetings.'

Emma saw her father whiten with fury and was glad to be despatched to the kitchen to provide them all with coffee. The hatch was open a crack. She risked widening the gap another inch, praying that the door would not creak.

As she expected, she had become their topic of conversation. The policeman slightly mollified her father by enquiring about her interests and seeming to accept the truth of his boast that she had had great difficulty choosing her A-level subjects since she would have been perfectly capable of coping with any.

When he asked whether she had a part in *A Midsummer Night's Dream,* her father became even more expansive. Emma cringed as she listened. He was talking as though Hermia were the main part, the rest of the cast having only minor supporting roles. He obviously knew nothing at all about the plot. Emma prayed that the policeman didn't either.

He had moved on to talk about the charity walk. 'I'm surprised Emma wasn't walking for such worthy causes.' Her parents spoke together, and, with the politeness he showed to her before strangers, her father gave way to her mother. 'She's not strong and it's a ridiculously long way.'

'A lot of them managed it with no trouble.'

Her father, his courtesy soon exhausted, cut the policeman off. 'Yes, a lot of undesirables, out for a night's rowdiness. I know the walk's well supervised, Officer, but Emma might have begun an association with someone who...well, wouldn't fit in.' Emma blushed for him and willed the sergeant to end his conversation and go.

She passed the coffee tray through the hatch and walked round to rejoin them. She found her mother worrying at a mark on the carpet, revealed when she had moved a small table. In spite of the officer's presence, she regarded Emma reproachfully and began another of her oblique attacks.

'I won't ask you if your friends have been in wrecking the place while we were away because I don't want to make you lie to me.' Emma resented this imputed dishonesty. The accusation was indirect only because her mother liked to air her grievances without risking a confrontation. 'I'll just remind you that my housekeeping is not of a standard where a chipped vegetable knife and a wine-stained cloth in the soiled linen will go unnoticed. And goodness knows what you've been wheeling across the carpet, crushing the pile and leaving muddy smears. Still, we'll talk about it later.' Emma knew they would not. Her mother wished merely to record her grievance before witnesses.

Hunter drained his coffee cup quickly. 'I'd like a few words with your daughter alone, if you wouldn't mind.'

Saxby bridled. 'I certainly would mind. You don't seem to know the limits of your own powers. You're not allowed to interview minors except in the presence of their parents.'

Hunter smiled, thinly. 'That's almost right, sir, but you need to check up your definition of a minor. Emma's seventeen and if you refuse your permission for me to interview her in these familiar surroundings, then I shall have to take her down to the station.'

Saxby walked to the door and silently held it open as his wife crept out. He followed her and closed it quietly.

To give the girl a few seconds to collect herself, Hunter strolled to the window and looked out. A garden stretched some sixty or seventy yards before him. Its lawns and beds had been elaborately laid out and expensively planted but they seemed at the moment to be suffering from slight neglect. The gardener's annual holiday, perhaps.

When he turned round again, Emma was surveying him. He ignored her and studied the room. Its lines were elegant, the ceiling mouldings beautiful and its total effect depressing. It contained a haphazard arrangement of artifacts meant, he supposed, to make some kind of cultural impact. They included a Mabel Lucie Atwell print and an elaborately carved piece of wood that he did not understand the import of but was impressed by. Surely no one would have laboured over such intricacies unless they had some significance.

A large coffee machine announced that the family seldom resorted to instant, although that was all he himself had merited. A cruet had been left on the table. These people ground their own peppercorns and rock salt and stored them in lead crystal. The couch and table top were covered in Liberty prints of which his own wife would have approved. A tree of Hornsea pottery mugs stood beside the cruet.

Too many vogues were married uneasily and the setting for them was botched. The walls were unevenly covered in too few coats of paint in an acid, stomach-curdling yellow against a carpet of hot mustard, now, mercifully, a little stained and faded. The contents of the alcove of shelves were a curious mixture of coffee-table picture books and genuine treasures with lovingly tooled bindings. The general impression was of an up-market salesroom.

He turned back to Emma who had dropped her gaze. 'What I told your parents wasn't news to you, was it? How did you know what had happened to Miss Feather?'

'Helen rang me.'

'But you didn't tell your parents what she said?'

She shook her head briefly. 'I decided to put off receiving the benefit of my father's opinion about it.'

'And his plan to take you away from your school?'

'Not that. He's always saying it but it doesn't mean anything. He can't afford to pay these days and they couldn't do better for a state school in Cloughton.'

Hunter nodded in acknowledgement. 'Did your friend say where she got her information?'

'From Daniel.'

Hunter sighed quietly. He had followed chains like this before. 'And who did you ring to pass on the news?'

She looked up at him, warily. 'A boy called Michael Cunningham.'

He noticed her discomfiture and changed the subject. 'What was the real reason you didn't do the walk, Emma? It strikes me your father would have appreciated such an exhibition of your public spirit.'

He could see that his tone had given her a gleam of hope that he understood her position. Apparently she decided to trust him. 'Michael Cunningham.'

'Your father didn't approve of him?'

'That's one way of putting it. But we'd finished together, anyway.'

'So, how did you spend the weekend?'

This time she actually smiled. 'You won't tell?'

'Not unless you're going to confess to something I'd have to arrest you for.'

She got up and took his place at the window, speaking to him over her shoulder.

'They left early on Saturday morning. I was supposed to be staying with my aunt. She's my godmother and my father's sister. Mother suspected that I wouldn't be but she never does more than hint and nag at me.

'Aunt Laura thinks it's time I had more independence. She told me to ring if I needed anything but, otherwise, she'd keep out of my way. I was to ring her to be collected any time up to midnight on Sunday when she'd want to lock up and go to bed.'

'And your parents were to think you'd been living there?'

She nodded. 'They got back at about one this morning. Their plane was due into Manchester at ten minutes to midnight. Aunt Laura thought I should stand up more to my parents but she knew I daren't face my father if I hadn't obeyed him. She says it wouldn't be any good if she spoke up for me. I need to do it myself.'

'She sounds a sensible lady. When was the arrangement made for Miss Feather to collect you before rehearsal yesterday?'

Emma looked startled, evidently having thought the interview was drawing to a close. She perched on the arm of a chair to explain. 'We had her last lesson on Friday. She kept me a minute at the end. She said she'd like a word with me and we could have it on the way to school on Sunday afternoon.'

'What about?'

Emma shrugged. 'Well, she didn't say but I assumed it was to do with the play, something I wasn't doing right. She'd told me before that my Hermia was a bit too hang-dog, that I'd got to put some more rebellion into it.'

'Couldn't she have told you there and then?'

Emma looked shocked. 'Oh no, she never criticized anybody in front of the others and the crowd was waiting outside in the corridor for me and listening.'

She slid guiltily on to the chair seat, obviously remembering parental admonitions about ruining the furniture. 'I hung on for her, just thinking something had held her up. I didn't know what to do. I'd be in trouble with Miss Feather if she came to collect me and I'd gone.'

'And in bother with Mr Naylor and company if you didn't turn up at the rehearsal on time.'

Emma's nose wrinkled. 'Not him, but I

knew Mrs Travers was coming to watch. She wouldn't listen to any excuses. Then the phone rang and it was Mr Naylor, but it was Miss Deakin who came to fetch me, thank goodness. I saved as much time as I could by going down the drive and waiting at the gate but she was still a bit short with me and it wasn't my fault.'

As she described this unfairness, Hunter heard just an echo of the mother's querulous passivity.

Browne had warned his team that their interviewees might be unavailable. Many of them would still be asleep after their labours of love for the less fortunate. Even those who were up again were likely to be stiff, cross, disorientated and generally unhelpful. Mitchell was neither surprised nor too disappointed, therefore, when there was no answer to his two jabs at the Travers' doorbell.

As he turned away he noticed a woman in the neighbouring garden, busy tying her faded narcissi leaves into bundles so that they could wither tidily. He nodded to her approvingly and she came to the hedge. 'Mr and Mrs Travers have gone for a walk,' she told him.

He blinked. 'I beg your pardon?'

She repeated the information and, when her word was still apparently doubted, she took offence. 'They went out ten minutes ago wearing anoraks and tatty tracksuit bottoms. He had boots on and she had shiny new trainers. He was carrying a little day sack. Of course, they might have been going to a cocktail party, but, somehow...'

Mitchell soothed her, then went off to buy himself a cup of coffee and decide on alternative plans for the afternoon.

Being veteran walkers, Kit and David Travers had completed their twenty miles safe from injuries or blisters and in the respectable time of five and a quarter hours. They had then slept the sleep of the justifiably weary, till the sun, in an apology for the ill-mannered weather of the night, had dazzled them awake through their south-facing bedroom window. Both of them led busy lives, which allowed only occasionally for twenty miles to be covered at a stretch and both of them rose rather stiffer than they were prepared to admit.

Kit had not been surprised when, as she

prepared lunch and the weather continued cool but sunny, Dave had begun to cast glances in the direction of his second and dry pair of walking boots. 'What about a gentle stroll when we've eaten? What kills cures, you know.' Kit resigned herself to the inevitable. She might as well walk some more. She hated sitting about during the last day of a holiday, feeling it evaporate round her as she tried to decide on the best way to spend it. Anyway, a walk might take her mind off things. She went to stand with him by the window.

'It's ideal conditions for tackling Stainwood Pike.' He knew he was pushing his luck.

'All weather is ideal for tackling some uphill journey, according to you. It's also ideal for an afternoon's gardening or painting the front bedroom. When it's hot you go on about the clear views and when it's filthy wet you say it's going to clear or it'll keep us cool.' Their amicable wrangling continued as she filled a flask with coffee and he packed waterproofs. 'I suppose you don't know any flat walks. Why do we always have to go up?'

'You can't get out of Cloughton without—and it's probably something to do
with the world being such an intimidating
place. We look at the high peaks of it and
somehow feel that if we can get them
under our feet we're still on top of things
in every other sense.'

He loved being on the tops. It made
Kit want to giggle when they walked
in the Lake District and he introduced
his companions to mountain peaks with
proprietorial pride, like a woman showing
visitors round her new house. 'You ooh
and aah about snow-capped hills on
the horizon and to me they look like
ridiculous iced buns against the sky. And
I've never understood the strange human
habit of giving personal names to chance
creasing, folding, melting and hardening of
an assortment of minerals.'

'I get the message. You aren't interested
in mountains.'

'How can you be interested or not
interested? They're just there.'

'That's why Hillary climbed Everest.'

'Then more fool him. The town hall's
there but I don't go climbing up to the
top of it.'

They had waved to their gardening

neighbour and set off in the direction of Stainwood. Heather had used to mean to her a sea of pink mist over a bleak moor beside a favourite road, reached by a pleasant drive. Since her first day on the moors with Dave it had been associated with a curious, high-stepping walk, lifting the legs clear over tufted roots, which soon led to trembling exhaustion.

Fortunately, the band of heather below Stainwood was narrow and her legs obeyed her as she reminded herself of the calories she was burning. She'd read somewhere that the metabolism remained raised for some time after vigorous exercise. She hoped it was true and consulted Dave about it. He shook his head. 'Not really my field. I'm just a humble dealer in chicken pox and sore throats.'

'Oh well, it doesn't matter. Walking with you doesn't qualify as sustained aerobic exercise. You're always stopping for long conferences with the map. I don't know why you bother looking for the route. You never follow it. Your idea of a path is the shortest distance between where you are and where you want to be—so long as it passes through at least one quagmire, one acre of nettles and a field with a bull. By the way, when does a bullock become a bull and how does it know when to modify its behaviour?'

'Really, Kit! You're not serious? Anyway, your idea of a path has three lanes and a central reservation so we only even one another up. Tell you what, pounding along on those hard surfaces did my knees a power of no good.'

Kit was unsympathetic. 'I enjoyed the road walking. I got into a rhythm that I could keep up for the whole distance with no interruptions to climb stiles or skirt round bogs or consult maps.'

Dave waved the map at her. 'It's a good job I do the navigating. You're happy just turning right at the next sheep.' He wandered happily ahead, turning from time to time with a 'Just look at...' or 'Did you see...?' She forbore to tell him that she seldom, when out walking with him, raised her eyes from the dubious ground directly in front of her to which she was required to trust her foot. Because of this method of progress, she often, as now, realized that they had reached the summit of the current hill only when Dave threw himself on to the turf with a sigh of satisfaction. 'What a view!'

When he slipped his arm round her shoulders, she stiffened. 'What's wrong? Have I upset you? You were joking all the way up.' He searched her face, perplexed.

'I can cope with joking. Just don't start kissing. I don't know what we're doing up here anyway. There's a funeral to arrange.'

'I think you'll find that won't be allowed for a while yet. I was hoping to take your mind off all that. I know Julia had come to mean a lot to you.'

Kit wriggled away to leave clear daylight between them. 'No she didn't. Until recently she was someone on the Christmas card list, an unfortunate relative we should be kind to. When I had the chance to do her a kindness, finding her that job in my department, I found she didn't need favours at all. All she means to me is a bizarre production of a well-known Shakespeare play and the edge to my colleagues' voices when they talk about "your cousin".'

He allowed the physical distance between them to remain. 'It's not like you to store up petty grievances.'

'What about the affair she was having with you? Was that petty?' She scrambled to her feet and set off down the slope towards Cloughton. Her husband hastened after her. She began to weep only when she tripped over a jutting stone and landed in an ungainly heap in his path.

Chapter 7

Adrian Naylor appeared worried when he answered Jennie's ring at his door. Obsequiously welcoming, he ushered her into a homely living kitchen and offered her a list of refreshments from which to choose. His tongue was as busy as his hands as he explained his predicament.

'You'll have heard about Fi's problem by now, I expect. I'm afraid she's rushed off into the lounge to avoid you.' He punctuated his nervous monologue with little feminine adjustments to the kitchen arrangements. 'She hates people to know what's wrong with her but I told her I'd have to tell you. Otherwise, in this situation, you might suspect all kinds of weird things.'

Jennie sympathized quite sincerely. 'It's

a wretched affliction for both of you.'

He smiled gratefully and presented her with the tea she had selected. 'It does make life a bit complicated. When Fi first moved in she was still managing to go to work but she can't face it any more. Not that it matters to me. I'm glad to be able to support her, but it was good for her to do it.'

'What does she do?'

'She's a nurse, a good one. It's the travelling she can't cope with more than the tasks she has to do when she gets there. Real emergencies take her out of herself. I wish I was free to provide transport but one of us has to have regular money coming in.' He paused to brush a few grains of sugar from the tray cloth. Jennie wondered, unkindly, whether he had embroidered the flowers on it himself.

'Letting her talk is another way I can help. It lowers her stress level to put her fears and frustrations into words, but she worries that I'll find it wearing to listen over and over. Julia helped a lot. She was a new audience whose patience hadn't been exhausted—but in the end Fi found her a liability. She wouldn't let Fi control her own life.' Jennie made a jotting in her notebook and Naylor looked alarmed. 'Are you taking all this down?'

'Some of it. You want my colleagues to understand too.'

Reassured, he continued. 'People are often very unkind. A lot of them think Fi is lazy and even those who've been told what the trouble is keep urging her to snap out of it. It doesn't help that the symptoms vary so much. One evening she'll enjoy visiting a friend and the next the very idea of going out makes her physically sick. The people she has to put off are offended, of course, and say she can manage it when she really wants to.'

Jennie watched him playing with a spoon, twisting it in his fingers, and decided that his own stress level, whatever that meant, was pretty high.

'Last week she dashed home from her parents' anniversary dinner and it's still making waves. And shopping is a nightmare. Recently I had to go out and buy her some new underwear.' He blushed crimson at the remembered embarrassment. 'I'd hoped Julia would do it but, by then, Fi had turned against her. Still, I shouldn't mind little things like that. If Fi were fit and well she wouldn't have chosen to live with someone like me.' His eyes implored Jennie to contradict him.

To avoid the appeal, she turned to less ephemeral matters. He answered her questions readily. 'I hadn't seen Julia since the end of school on Friday but she did ring yesterday to make sure Fi would still be walking.'

Now he had Jennie's full attention. 'Who spoke to her?'

'Both of us. I told her I'd do my best to make sure Fi turned up. I thought she'd be so pleased with herself if she managed it. It was in such a good cause and she's often better if she's concerned with something or someone else. It distracts her. And if she has to go out, she finds the dark easier than the daylight. It was the wind that did for her. She doesn't like wind. She says it's "feely".'

He offered more tea and Jennie accepted, hoping further information would flow with it. 'Is Fiona all you talked about?'

He looked crestfallen. 'Yes, then I passed the receiver over but Fi wouldn't talk to her. She only said she'd do her best and put the phone down.'

'What time was this?'

'Just before twelve, as far as I can remember.'

'After church?'

'Yes.' He nodded. 'She said she'd just come from there and was on her way out to lunch.'

'Who with? I thought you said you only talked about Fiona!'

He bit his lip like a naughty schoolboy and Jennie moderated her tone. 'Did she say? And where was she ringing from?'

He sat silent, hearing Julia's voice over again in his head before answering carefully. 'She said she couldn't chat because Andrew hated to be kept waiting. I didn't ask where she was and I'm certain she didn't say.' He could offer no information about any Andrew. Reluctantly, Jennie decided she could no longer put off forcing her attentions on the feeble Fiona.

Mitchell sat in the back-street 'caff' to which he retired whenever his life was in need of review and amendment. He had been surprised to find it open on a Bank Holiday, but, as its fat proprietress explained, it was her 'window on life, the family having all moved away' and, since the other places of refreshment were shut, trade was ticking over nicely.

She had, she told him, learned almost all she knew from listening to her customers' conversation. From Mitchell, she had learned to think that a moderate amount of free 'vittling' for certain officers of the law was a small price to pay for the shops in Cloughton being able to flourish free from the attentions of villains.

She fished for details of the robbery from the unfortunate Mr Mason in the precinct. Catching nothing, she sniffed. 'Prime locations for trade is prime locations for thieving. I do all right in me back-street, thanks very much.' She slapped a plate of toasted current teacake in front of Mitchell after flicking a hot soapy cloth over the table's plastic top, then surveyed him, her head on one side. 'Cheer up, it might never 'appen.'

Mitchell winked at her. 'I've already made it happen. My tongue's too long and I give it too much exercise.'

This amused her. 'Aye, you an' me both.'

When Mitchell looked again she was back behind the counter. He wondered how she had inveigled her ample hips between the closely packed tables without disturbing them, then returned to his self-examination.

Why did he give Hunter so much stick? He didn't dislike the man basically and he was a good copper. It was just that he asked to be ribbed. If he gave as good as he got when he was teased, Mitchell would leave him alone. He'd better watch it, though. As his CI's son-in-law he could expect to get stamped on even harder than the others if—or rather when—he stepped out of line.

On the whole, he was getting on reasonably well with his father-in-law. Declan helped. Now he was an engaging though unbeautiful eight-month-old his parents had been forgiven for the disgrace of his unplanned conception. The wedding had been quite a good do in the end, though the christening had caused some sticky moments. Browne had had mixed feelings about attending a Catholic baptism to witness his daughter's offspring being given an Irish name, though they had disarmed him by adding his own. Declan Thomas sounded well and everyone was pleased, except perhaps his own father. Still, he wasn't saddling a son of his with

Bernard to please anyone.

He'd overheard Browne making a few face-saving growling noises to Hannah. 'All that fuss about the child being brought up a Catholic! I'd be totally in sympathy if they were Mass-every-Sunday, no-meat-on-Friday types. I could respect that—but they're just being aggressively Irish. Not that Benny shows many of the traits usually attributed to the Irish. His accent's as Yorkshire as mine and he's certainly not laid back or lazy. He's true to form in his drinking habits, though.' Since Browne had been disposing of his second pint of Mitchell's best bitter as he made these remarks, they seemed a mite unfair.

Back in the present, he repressed a shudder and told himself he really did like tea without sugar—or he would, once he got used to it. Such a lot of things had changed lately. Jennie Smith had taken the plunge a month or two after Ginny and himself. It still felt odd to call her Taylor. Maybe he wouldn't be calling her anything at all for much longer—in working hours at least. From the way she was drooling over Declan last week, she might well be the next one to leave them.

Hardly any of the old team were working

on this case. Richard was busy with the chemist's break-in. Robin Carson was jabbing computer buttons, learning how to construct photofit faces from witnesses' descriptions. And he could still hardly believe that old Nigel had defected to the uniformed lot—and in Barrow-in-Furness of all places! Was being promoted to sergeant worth that?

He looked up at a shout from behind the counter. 'You lot have got a body on your hands, haven't you?' He hushed his benefactress, though the shop was now empty. 'Haven't you got work to do?' He folded the last piece of teacake into his mouth and stood up with a sigh.

'I can't find the people I should be interviewing. I can't speak to my boss—he's at the mortuary. If I choose my own job for the afternoon I'm in trouble. If I waste it in here I'm in trouble—from you as well...'

She clattered his pots on to her tray. 'If you can't please the gaffer, you might as well please yourself.'

Mitchell thought this was good advice.

Though he had no doubts about his ability to cope with it, DC Richard Dean had been surprised when Browne left the investigation at Mason's entirely in his hands. He was pleased by his progress, though his pleasure in it was a little marred by the discovery of the body on the canal bank and the ensuing murder investigation from which his present duties kept him.

He had used his initiative, worked hard and got a long way. The drugs missing from the chemist's vandalized cabinet were amphetamines, certainly Class B drugs, and Class A if they were prepared for injection. It could be fourteen years for his customer when he'd caught him. In the intervals of following up his clues and his hunches, he had buried himself away to read up on the uses and abuses of bennies, dennies, uppers and speed.

He had been familiar with the slang terms. Now he knew a bit about what they were and what they did. He was looking for restless, irritable behaviour, alternating moods of elation and depression, lack of tact and discretion, thirst, a dry mouth and bad breath. Perhaps he had discovered the secret of what made Superintendent Petty the great man they all knew him to be!

Loss of appetite and weight was standard—no, forget the Super. A bright-eyed look was typical and photophobia—large pupils and a fear of bright lights that might lead to the wearing of dark glasses.

He had tried visiting the two Cloughton night spots most favoured by its younger elements but the music was too loud to overhear much conversation and the lighting too intermittent to look for the physical symptoms. Then the idea of drug-assisted sport had occurred to him, and the possible usefulness of being a spectator at the Cloughton Couriers' Bank Holiday frolics that had been advertised in the *Clarion*.

He had enjoyed himself. There had been fun races first for the very young and he had sat at the end of a bench in front of a white-painted sight screen and watched them cavorting over the faded white lines of three of last year's wickets in the centre of a four-hundred-metre track.

As the field darkened slightly, the serious runners warmed up, the furthest away visible only as silver flashes of the reflective material on their garments. They milled about the field, walking in circles, doing stretching exercises and massaging their calf muscles. The younger of them wore designer gear and eyed each other's outfits with contempt or envy. Dean found he could easily recognize the sex of each silhouette by its gait. They were all much too absorbed to be interrupted. He moved towards the club hut.

'Please remove spikes before entering' the door politely requested. He decided no exception could be taken to his Reebok trainers and went in. He walked past an uncomfortable-looking park-type bench, with slatted seat and back and a brass plaque commemorating a past member, and seated himself on an armless chair with a tubular frame. The seating was so varied that he wondered if each member had been asked to make a contribution from the spares at home.

Reared against the wall, a brightly painted notice read SLOW RUNNERS ON ROAD and beside it a pile of second-hand strip lighting waiting to be fixed. Meanwhile, four unshaded, fly-specked bulbs did service. There was a kitchen corner with a sink, drainer and a large urn. A counter in front for serving was covered in paper cups. Dean began to feel thirsty but there was no sign of activity yet in that area and the urn was not humming.

He wandered over to a huge notice board, headed with the club's name and logo. It contained the notices he had expected—items for sale, a demand for subs to be paid, an instruction to WEAR BRIGHT CLOTHING. Reports of all ventures and competitions ended uniformly with sanguine speculations. There were various very good sharp action photographs. Someone had a professional camera.

As the time for the road race departure approached the hut became more crowded. There was a damp grass smell that Dean associated with summer camping and a total absence of cigarette smoke. As the runners grumbled about the *Clarion's* biased reporting of Cloughton sport with its emphasis on ball games, he had his first opportunity to examine their faces. He found none of the features he was looking for.

Dean understood that the dead girl had been a member here but he heard no mention of her demise. All the chatter was of times and races, until, after numerous hushings, the coach addressed them. Throughout his encouraging remarks, various conversations continued round the edges of the room. Then it was time for off and the room cleared quickly. Dean found himself sitting beside an expensively tracksuited man of about forty and set about trying to collect information from him. A solicitor who had taken a St John's Ambulance course, he had been recruited as the club's first aid officer and was more than happy to fill in his spell of duty chatting about its affairs.

'The club's existed for more than a hundred years and a year or two ago our numbers grew enormously with the great running boom. It's coming to an end now. A few will stay but we're getting back to normal.'

'You're pleased about that?'

He nodded. 'Running, for busy people, often has to be done at unsociable hours. An incidental bonus is solitude. We lost it for a while but we're getting it back now the craze people are defaulting.'

'You run...for *relaxation?*'

He nodded. 'Yes, it's not on the whole a competitive sport. There are races, of course, but what you're up against is just your own last record, your Personal Best, and your fellow runners are your allies—unless you're young Daniel, of course. I suppose his school pushes him towards sporting excellence and success.' He flipped up the lid of his first aid box and did a silent check of its contents, before continuing his monologue.

'Not that I'm convinced that the two are the same. It's obviously right to be physically fit but we've taken races and competitions and challenges that measure the fitness and made them an end in themselves. And that's made us less fit, both mentally and physically.' The contents of his box of medicaments had obviously satisfied him. Now he faced Dean with a fixed stare and the DC had difficulty dragging his own gaze away.

'We get depressed when something takes us a second longer or someone does it a second faster. We rely on emaciation and technique for the last ounce of speed. We live unnatural lives. Hours of rigorous and misdirected training distorts normality and we call it being disciplined and dedicated.'

Dean felt breathless for him but agreed with the general gist of his argument. The solicitor smiled at his own vehemence. 'Of course, whatever the level of speed or commitment, the problems achieving our aims are the same for everybody. That accounts for our fellowship and also for our interminable boring conversation. That, and having little else in common.

When we meet for social events it's always awkward. The binding activity is not in progress.'

He abandoned his social philosophy to air a personal grudge. 'Organization isn't easy either. A lot of the officials here are volunteers who can enjoy power nowhere else. Capable people are prevented from offering their services because of the impossible job of liaising with incompetents.'

Now Dean understood why the man had been sitting alone amidst the crowd. He wondered where in the social scale this snobbish keep-fit lawyer would place a detective constable.

He looked around for more congenial company and was astonished to see a bulky form huddled in a corner, attempting the impossible task of looking inconspicuous. 'Whatever are you doing here? You're never going to attempt to run off that beer-belly!'

Mitchell came out of his corner. 'No, I came along with Wonder Boy who ran the town walk, but apparently he's inexhaustible. He's gone off to run some more.'

'Tough.'

Mitchell shrugged. 'Doesn't matter. I'd

finished my chat with him, at least for the moment. I'm hanging around though till the coach comes back. He was some sort of friend of the dead woman. What about you? Didn't know you were a runner.'

'I'm not.' Dean sat down on a plastic chair and Mitchell reluctantly trusted his weight to the one beside it. He explained the purpose of his own visit while the solicitor eyed them both curiously. 'There's a young lad works Saturdays at Mason's. He's not here tonight. I don't think he exerts himself much but I've been sniffing round him and his friends. Just a minute...'

He wandered over to examine more closely one of the photographs pinned to the board, an enlarged snapshot of a group of boys, laughing and disco dancing in the clubroom with balloons and streamers above them. 'I was right. He does come here with his mates, for the social events at least.'

He looked across at the first aider. 'Excuse me, this boy in the middle of the group here, it's Michael Cunningham, isn't it?' It was confirmed by an unenthusiastic nod.

Mitchell beamed. 'Welcome aboard, Richard. Your lad might not be much

140

of a mover but he's your ticket back to the murder team.'

The two officers compared detailed notes whilst the hut was being prepared for the runners' return. A lady came in, switched on the urn and lined up jars of 'chews' and plates of biscuits. Parents drifted in and chatted, waiting to escort their youngsters home. They were mostly overweight and slack-muscled. Mitchell muttered in Dean's ear, 'Have they brought their offspring here so they won't end up looking the same or is that what muscles turn to when training stops?'

Dean poked Mitchell's ample middle. 'At least your belly doesn't wobble.' Sniggering, they separated and mingled with the accumulating crowd. Blisters and sprains were being shown off proudly. The evening cooled and darkened and the hot liquid from the urn steamed up the windows.

Mitchell found a youth who claimed to be Michael's friend. As he answered questions, he tore off pieces from a currant loaf and chewed them and Mitchell forced himself not to step backwards from the reeking, sweating body. 'Michael's not a runner, only a jogger.'

'What's the difference?'

The youth shrugged disparagingly. 'He's never done an eight-minute mile or entered a race or taken the whole thing seriously. He doesn't keep at it—has lay-offs for months on end. I don't know why he started coming.'

'When did he?'

Another shrug. 'About this time last year, I think. You want to know a lot. You the fuzz?'

Mitchell acknowledged it, first to the youth and then, after a quick consultation with Dean, by an announcement to the whole gathering. The atmosphere immediately became subdued and grieving, as though the preceding merriment had not happened. Mitchell was sorry to spoil it. 'I don't want to put the damper on your Bank Holiday. I'm sure Julia wouldn't have wanted that. If you were one of the walkers you'll be seen by one of our team very soon. For now, I just want to ask anyone who knows anything that might throw some light on what happened to her yesterday to come and speak to us.'

As he had expected, Mitchell was besieged by teenagers anxious to be part of the enquiry, but, with Dean's assistance and their parents' wish to put an end to a long and tiring day, they were seen and despatched in no more than an hour. He glanced at his watch and then at Andrew Metcalfe, their remaining witness. 'We've all deserved a pint and the weight off our feet.' Needing no further encouragement, the Courier followed him across the road.

In the Drum and Monkey, they sat round a small table and allowed Metcalfe to talk about his coaching. 'Just watch kids in a playground. They're in perpetual motion. They don't move very fast and they pause from time to time but they keep on the go. I seldom have to waste much time on basic conditioning.' He looked pointedly at Mitchell. 'Kids are already in shape.'

Mitchell stuck his nose in his glass and stopped listening. He'd be playing cricket all summer, wouldn't he? And if he had let the pounds creep on over the winter, you couldn't insult a new wife's cooking, especially when it was as bad as Ginny's. Anyway, he had stopped taking sugar in his tea. He drank deeply.

Metcalfe had moved on. 'When I send them off to take their LSD I'm not talking about money or acid. It's their

Long Steady Distance.' He'd made this joke many times and waited for their laughter. Dean, though, was looking at him hard. 'Sorry. I'm getting off the point. You wanted me to tell you about Julia. She hadn't done any running before she came to Cloughton and she took to it well. Drop-outs try it, do one or two test work-outs, discover it can be painful and stop. It takes six to eight weeks to get over the first hump of pain but then you get to the encouraging part. Julia did well, though, saw it through.'

Both officers did their best to look fascinated, then Dean collected their glasses and escaped to the bar, leaving Mitchell to hear more. 'Competitive runners measure their improvement in tenths of a second but beginners improve dramatically even day by day. Julia was interested in the mental aspect. I was telling her one night that running was therapeutic in depression. It's time out from all your current problems and possibly it causes chemical changes in the brain. She said she had a friend who might be helped that way. She never brought her down to the club though.'

He nodded to Dean in acknowledgement of his fresh pint. 'I tell my beginners that moving slowly is faster than standing still.'

Mitchell was getting desperate. 'What can you tell us about Julia over the past week?'

'We had lunch together yesterday. It was here as a matter of fact, so you won't have to go far to check up. We met early, about half past twelve, because she had to go to school in the afternoon. We left here at about one fifteen. I went down the road to the club to do some interval training myself. Julia went up to school.'

'No she didn't. What exactly was your relationship with her?'

'I never exactly knew.' His tone showed that he resented this aspect of their questions.

'She's dead. She's been killed. I need to know about her.'

He nodded. 'Sorry. But it's true that I didn't know where I stood. She was a looker, a bit of a swinger and definitely a good sport in many ways. I was attracted to her physically and we'd been seen around together. I'd even been to church with her—and there's the rub. She was a deadly earnest Catholic. Wouldn't discuss contraception, wouldn't even think about

145

abortion. I was afraid she was beginning to see me as husband material, that I'd have to marry her to get any more than a hug and a kiss. I was trying to cool it a bit, except that, in the usual sense, it hadn't got hot.'

'Thank you. And she actually said when she left you that she was going to school?'

He nodded solemnly.

Dean's impatience had become almost tangible. 'Can I ask you about the misuse of drugs in sport?'

He was taken aback at the sudden change of subject. When he adjusted, they saw that they had lost his goodwill again. 'You can, but you'll not find it amongst the Couriers and I don't know much about it.'

Their relief was short-lived. The little he knew lasted throughout the next pint: 'Beta-blockers... bronchospasm...impurities... black market... IAAF wants random testing right through the year but the cost would be huge...five to fifteen times the medical dose...black bombers...pillheads...'

'Your shout,' Mitchell announced and watched triumphantly as Metcalfe got up to stand his round. 'So,' he summarized in the expert's absence, 'anabolic steroids are used as training drugs. Stimulants that we're interested in are used at the event. Looks like we could be following his little dears to their next race meeting.'

Metcalfe got his three pints just as last orders were called. He set them carefully on the table. 'Funny you being so interested in all that drug business,' he remarked as he repossessed his stool. 'That's all Julia's wanted to talk about for the last couple of weeks.'

Chapter 8

Browne raised his eyebrows as he surveyed the officers who had reported for his Tuesday morning briefing. 'Obviously there's some good reason for Richard being among us. Doubtless I shall hear it in due course. Meanwhile, I'll begin with the incontrovertible evidence before we start floating fanciful theories.'

They arranged themselves as comfortably as they could whilst he picked up the post mortem report. 'We now have a formal confirmation of murder by stabbing. The entry wound was just a slit so the weapon was sharp. Ledgard thinks, though he doesn't commit himself, that it had only a single cutting edge. He's uncertain because of fibres from thick clothing embedded in the skin. There was no rocking or twisting of the weapon to tear the slit open.

'So she didn't struggle or wriggle away.' Only Mitchell would have dared to interrupt the reading of a PM report, and even he looked abashed and quickly subsided again.

'Ledgard thinks the weapon was left in the wound and only withdrawn a considerable time after death so there wouldn't have been much external bleeding even at the time. The wound was about six inches deep and, at the point of entry, just over one inch across, so that's the size of the blade we're after. It was inserted with considerable force and struck a glancing blow to the rib. A minute fragment of metal was found in the soft tissue.

'There was no bruising in the surface tissues so Julia was obviously taken by surprise and died before she could struggle.' He regarded Mitchell sardonically. 'Ledgard will be glad of your confirming agreement. The surface wound looked trival.'

148

Browne began to gather the sheets of the report together, then looked at the top one again. 'One arm was bent at a right angle in rigor. The other possibly had been but it was broken at the elbow after death, probably as the body was in transit—being pushed into a car boot, maybe. We're sure the body was moved after the stabbing. The SOCO didn't find the faintest smear of blood on the ground and there had to be at least a little. We knew rigor seemed fully established when the body was found at eight o'clock. When Ledgard began the PM at two thirty, it was passing from the face, jaw and neck. He tells me we can't read too much into this. Strong muscles stiffen later and remain in rigor longer than old or feeble ones. The cold slows it down too. He suggests the region of two o'clock on Sunday afternoon as the time of death—not after that anyway.'

Again Mitchell made as if to speak, then thought better of it. Browne paused mockingly, waiting for his permission to continue. 'Julia's car, by the way, has been found in the car park of the Red Lion in Granby Road, about a quarter of a mile from the school, a red Fiat.' He gave them the registration. 'We've sent it for examination but it's a bit pointless. She seems to have given lifts to all and sundry. Right, Benny, you obviously had something to confess.'

Mitchell explained his failure to locate the Travers pair and his choice of the Stevens family as an alternative. 'I didn't want to waste the afternoon and I couldn't get to you for alternative instructions.'

'That seems fairly sensible. I don't disapprove of all shows of initiative.'

Mitchell's face mirrored his disbelief, but he merely added, 'It was a sad sort of place, very clean and tidy. The woman's in the hospice so the house is the work of two men doing their best to make a home without knowing how. I suppose I should have gone back to see the Travers in the evening but young Daniel invited me to the Couriers' holiday evening races. I met Richard there.'

Browne turned to Dean. 'I'm glad to have my verbal hit-man back in harness, even temporarily.' Dean smirked and Mitchell wriggled uncomfortably. Dean had planned to say that they had gone to the Couriers' meeting for some exercise and met by chance, but he preferred defying his father-in-law to deceiving him. He felt relieved as Dean explained the actual purpose of his visit.

'There were a few things about this break-in that didn't add up. The shop's burglar alarm alerted a passing squad car very quickly. They were there a couple of minutes after it started and yet there'd been a great deal of damage done. Then, the glass from the broken panel was inside the shop, which you'd expect if someone had broken in from the ginnel but the SOCO said there were signs that it had been gathered up from the outside and moved in. Most peculiar of all, the hard stuff with the highest street value was still there in the cabinet.'

'So what had gone?'

'Amphetamines according to Mr Mason. He seemed a decent enough chap, very keen to tell me all about the security measures he takes. He has a boy he employs part-time, Saturday mornings and the odd weekday evening. I haven't been able to pin anything on to the lad but I didn't like the way it looked. If he was responsible, he doesn't seem to be on the stuff himself, so I was looking around amongst his associates for some of the physical signs of amphetamine abuse. I thought if I could find somebody he'd supplied, I might get the story out of him. Cunningham wasn't likely to cough. He's a hard case.'

'Cunningham?'

'That's right.' Mitchell could keep silent no longer. 'One of the boys in the school...'

'Where was he during the break-in?' Browne had not taken his eyes from Dean.

'He was supposed to be at a disco, Bertie's in Savile Street. I've found some youngsters who were dancing with him up to about half past nine, and then everyone who was there remembers him clowning around conspicuously towards the end. Nothing in between, though. The squad car got to the shop at ten twenty-eight.'

Browne looked up from his notebook. 'Was Cunningham trusted with any keys? And I suppose you've spoken to the doorman at Bertie's and the car park attendant.'

Dean nodded. 'They only notice if there's any rowdyism and they watch the kids coming in rather than going out.'

'I think I shall go and see your chemist, Richard.' Dean's face fell. 'No, the drugs investigation is still all yours but the boy

152

was in Julia Feather's play and rumour has it he was angling for some sort of relationship with her. I just want to borrow your witness to assist with our enquiry.'

'They might be all one, sir.' Between them, Dean and Mitchell gave an account of their discoveries the previous evening. Browne made copious notes, but showed none of the hoped for excitement.

'Right. Now Benny, what about your efforts with the Stevenses beforehand?'

Mitchell did not feel there was a great deal to report. 'It was difficult to get much out of Daniel. I couldn't put him at his ease. He kept tapping a pencil against the table top till I asked him to stop so then he twiddled the buttons on his jacket. He talked non-stop about every subject but the one I'd asked him about. He's a good-natured lad. I think he wasn't sure what would and what wouldn't get his friends into trouble, especially Michael. Though, I didn't get the impression that they were friends exactly. It was more that he seemed a bit afraid of him. It's odd because Daniel is certainly no wimp.

'I tackled him about Michael and Julia. He said Michael claimed to buy her drinks in his local pub. None of the others go in so they don't know if it's true. Metcalfe complained, though, that Michael was always hanging round her.'

'Mrs Stevens is an invalid, isn't she?'

'She's dying of cancer. She'd spent the weekend in the hospice and they were preparing to fetch her home again. By the way, Daniel said Emma Saxby was a member of the Couriers and last year she was a leading light in the school's athletics, the hundred and two hundred metres and the sprint relay. She trained through the winter for this season, then dropped out of the early meetings with a series of feeble excuses.

'The interesting thing I learned from them was this, though. When Fiona Manley was hiding behind her bush and screaming and Naylor was trying to get her back on the path, Neil Stevens and his mate went to see what the commotion was about. Naylor was saying she'd only a couple of hundred yards to go to get to Julia's car and she was yelling, "It won't be there! I know it won't be there!" '

'Did she now?'

'She might say that just in her general panic, I think.'

They turned to Jennie. Now that her

report about Julia's lunch date with Andrew Metcalfe had been upstaged, she felt that it had been full of negatives. She summarized her discussion with Naylor. 'I don't think he does Fiona any favours. He talks about her almost exclusively, with heavy emphasis on his sympathy and understanding. People are probably more fed up with that than they are with her. He said she'd talk to me in the front room if she didn't have to get out of her chair. I went through expecting some languishing character out of a sentimental nineteenth-century novel and found she was a forthright and shrewd and very pretty girl, though it was true she did seem to need to cling to that chair.

'She was by no means a neurotic non-entity. She seemed to despise herself far more than anyone else could scorn her. She was well aware that Adrian had a huge crush on Julia—said it was growing pains. She was terribly embarrassed by the exhibition she made of herself on Sunday night. The canal bank is a particularly bad place for her with no barriers at the water's edge. She told me about a child with a terrible physical disability who did the walk in callipers and then she said she actually envied him because he was unafraid and people accept him as he is. She hasn't seen a doctor. I think she's worried he'll tell her she's losing her mind. If I did nothing else that was useful, I think I may have talked her into consulting her GP.'

Browne had stopped taking notes but was listening with interest. The girl had evidently won Jennie over, and Jennie suffered no fools.

'She found it totally impossible to reason herself out of her horrors so she's used her brains to find practical ways to cope. She admitted to becoming quite a proficient liar to get away gracefully—you know, pulled muscles, forgotten letters and so on—and she's taken to alcohol. She doesn't get drunk but she takes a stiff drink before every ordeal. Oh, and she has a suitcase that she pushes or pulls along. She says it helps her stay in touch with reality and when she begins to feel giddy or unreal, it's something to hang on to.'

'She doesn't sound like a very reliable witness.'

Jennie shrugged and closed her notebook. 'That's all.'

'Any comments?' Browne looked round the team.

'Weird.'

'All very interesting but it doesn't get the case any further along.'

'Didn't you say she was a nurse? She'd know where to stick the knife.'

'Well, you did say Richard was the verbal hit-man.'

'So I did, Jerry. Go on, it's your turn.'

Hunter, too, felt he had nothing factual or practical to contribute. He gave the account of his conversation with the Saxby family.

'What did you think Emma would tell you without her family there?'

'Not a lot. I just didn't like Saxby's attitude and wondered if the girl would be any different away from him. They're a funny lot. I couldn't decide whether they were rich and shiftless or poor and struggling to impress. The mother certainly liked airing their unresolved grievances in front of a third party.' He looked at Browne. 'Did you get to church? Though I suppose it hardly matters now we know that Julia went off to lunch afterwards hale and hearty.'

Browne nodded. 'She was an exemplary, Mass-every-Sunday, no-meat-on-Friday member of Sacred Heart.'

Mitchell smiled to himself. Browne was

evidently proud of this succinct definition of a faith he did not share. Then he stopped smiling. He didn't really share it himself, except as a taken-for-granted background to his early life. He supposed that was all that the religious observances of his mother and the rest of the O'Brien clan meant to him. That, and having to suffer Benedict as his given name.

'Metcalfe told us that!' Dean leered. 'She was an exemplary, no-contraception, no-sex-before-marriage—member of the Couriers too. Of course, not all Catholics are so fussy.'

He smiled at Mitchell who clenched his fists in his pockets.

Browne asked quietly, 'Do you want to stay on this enquiry, Richard?' Without waiting for an answer, he began to summarize their findings. 'Ledgard thinks Julia was dead by two o'clock and, if Metcalfe is to be believed, she was still alive at one fifteen. We'd better check him over at the pub as he invited you to.' Mitchell indicated that he had already done so.

'She was wearing jeans and an anorak when we found her, sir. That's not the sort of thing I'd choose to wear to be taken out to lunch—well, not on a Sunday, anyhow—so she may well have gone back to the house to change.'

Browne acknowledged Jennie's point.

'Richard, you'll need to go back to Metcalfe for your own purposes so check up what she treated him to in the way of glamour. And, Jennie, see Hilary Deakin and ask if there were signs that Julia had been back for a quick change when she returned from her own lunch.'

'Sir.' Browne turned to Mitchell, amused. This form of address had been on his lips far more often since the wedding than it had ever been before. 'What if Hilary Deakin killed her before she set out for her rehearsal? She could have gone off to school herself and disposed of the body later.'

'Hilary Deakin had a lunch appointment of her own. She was being delivered to school—and she took Kit Travers back with her to the house afterwards.'

'She could have made an excuse to be dropped at home and dumped the body in the garage or something.'

'There isn't a garage.'

'Well, somewhere else then.'

Jennie said quietly. 'Sir, there was a

wheelchair in the little back porch. It used to belong to Miss Deakin's mother.'

Mitchell flashed her a grateful smile. 'There you are, sir. Julia's arms were bent at right angles when we found her, weren't they? As though she'd been sitting in a chair and resting them on its arms.'

'You're persistent, Benny, I'll say that for you. All right, Jennie. Find out the name of Miss Deakin's friend and where they ate and Benny can have the pleasure of checking out his own theory after he's finished the other jobs I've got lined up for him. Benny, you can see the Travers family, and don't get waylaid this time. She'll be at school and he'll be wherever busy GPs are by the middle of the morning, finishing a surgery most likely. You might have gained an advantage, seeing them separately.'

'Sir, am I to ask Miss Deakin how she knew it was a stabbing?'

Browne considered before shaking his head. 'Not if we can find out without. Have we picked up any clues about how this particular grapevine worked?'

'Neil Stevens told Daniel.'

'And Daniel rang Helen and Helen rang Emma and Emma rang Michael Cunningham.'

'It doesn't seem very likely that a pupil would have rung Miss Deakin, even Michael.'

'We'll go and ask him.' He turned to Dean. 'So, I need to borrow another of your witnesses. In fact, I'll go myself. I'd like to meet a teenager who's more than a match for you, Richard.'

'Was it just the news of Julia's death that gave rise to all this telephoning or was the method being passed round as well?' asked Hunter.

'Let's see what Helen heard and what she passed on. You can have that one, Jerry.'

Hunter nodded but had another suggestion. 'The school will be buzzing with gossip and they've got a play almost ready to perform. Advertising posters are up already and the tickets may well be printed.' Browne nodded. 'If they don't abandon the production, I'd like to find some excuse to attend a rehearsal. There would be a large collection of pupils and several staff all talking rather more freely than in a formal interview. It's not just what they might say. Warning or accusing glances sometimes tell us a lot.'

Jennie and Dean, their action sheets in

their hands, had drifted towards the door. Mitchell caught Browne's speculative eye on him and hurriedly turned his own on Hunter. 'I suggest an arty-farty officer to watch an arty-farty play.'

'Right, Benny.' Browne was angry at this unprovoked rudeness. 'We'll ask Jerry to go and, for your education, you'd better go with him.' Both men looked dismayed. 'Another minute, Jerry.' Taking this as dismissal, the rest departed.

Hunter, to Browne's surprise, was laughing. 'He just can't get out of the habit. He really tries to be sociable most of the time now, and then, suddenly his tongue runs away with him. But did you have to punish me as well? I don't think Benny and Shakespeare are going to like each other very much—not as he's represented in this play, anyway. I'm going to have to suffer his opinion of it all.'

Browne relented. 'Find out if and when the rehearsals are taking place and I'll see if I can't get him urgently called away. There are a few things I want to chew over. You free at lunchtime? I'll meet you in the Fleece at twelve thirty.' He began to tidy his desk. 'What I can't work out is how someone could have brought a body along the canal path either way with all those people passing through.'

Hunter paused in the doorway on his way out. 'In a wheelchair under cover of darkness? Maybe Benny's on to something.'

Since Helen would be in school, Hunter decided to pay a preliminary visit to her home. Having the goodwill of the Rowe parents could do no harm to his chances of obtaining information from their daughter. Compton Road ran at right angles to Willow Lane where the Saxbys lived. The Rowes' house was smaller, less imposing but much better maintained, its paint white and fresh and its garden trim. It was obviously the work of Mrs Rowe, who rose from her haunches in the border as he walked up the path. She was sensibly dressed in dark trousers and a cotton sweatshirt, slightly grubby, for which she made no apology.

She seated him in a slightly untidy living room as he explained his need to question Helen and her friends and his wish to reassure their parents. She nodded co-operatively as the telephone rang, then excused herself and picked up the receiver beside her. The caller spoke at some length, Mrs Rowe contributing the odd word. Her eyes apologized and Hunter hid his impatience. It was almost ten minutes before he had her attention again.

'You've met the Saxbys, haven't you? I don't know why she doesn't say it all to him. I can't do anything about it.'

'Husband trouble?'

'Well, it isn't all his fault. Both of them think their careers are important and each of them needs the other's support. They never listen to each other to resolve anything. They just have two monologues that never make a dialogue. She's one of life's grumblers. He's a perfectionist who expects everyone else to live up to his expectations of them. He's not flexible in adjusting to people's weaknesses or changing circumstances—and his social and economic aspirations are far loftier than his ability to achieve them. They used to be quite a close family, but now...'

She seemed oblivious of Hunter's tentative attempts to bring her back to his own business and he decided to let her give vent to her mingled concern and irritation. She'd concentrate better on his questions when she'd finished. 'Emma gets caught in the crossfire,' Mrs Rowe went on. 'Clare expresses her frustration over Derek in over-protectiveness of Emma and in ridiculously high hopes for her. Helen's asked me more than once to speak up for Emma to her parents, talk them into letting her join in more of the other young people's ordinary activities—the things they do just for fun—but if you want to stop someone being manipulated it's no use starting with the manipulators. I told Helen she could best help Emma by encouraging her to speak up for herself.' She laughed ruefully. 'What a dreadful gossip I am, but Clare irritates me. She goes around with a special look on her face that says, "You aren't really a lady but, don't worry, my Christian charity extends to everybody." '

Hunter laughed aloud. 'Yes, I've met her. I know what you mean, but I really must ask you what I came to ask. Helen heard about Miss Feather's death from Daniel Stevens, didn't she?' Mrs Rowe nodded. 'Did she tell you about it?' Another nod. 'What exactly did she say?'

She hesitated, trying to remember. 'She was in here with me. She hadn't been up long and she was putting dressings on her blisters. I was telling her the bathroom was the place for that but I hadn't the heart to insist. I could almost hear her muscles protesting when she moved. She picked up the receiver and told me it was Daniel and I went into the kitchen. I never listen in when he phones. She's of an age to value her privacy. She came in to me after a few minutes and I could see she was upset.'

'What exactly did she say?'

'I think she said, "Miss Feather's dead. Dan's father found her on the canal path." I said, "Don't be silly!" but it was just something to say. I actually believed it at once. Neil and Dan wouldn't pass on silly rumours.'

'Did she give any details—about what exactly had happened?'

She shook her head. 'No, we still don't know.' After a pause she went on carefully, 'I'm afraid she soon got over it and was on the phone to Emma, passing on the news and discussing what was going to happen about the play.'

'It's a funny time of year to do a school play, isn't it? What about exam preparations? Some of them have GCSEs and A-levels coming up in two or three weeks!'

'Those people aren't involved. Even if the performance had been in February as originally planned, the cast is all from the third and fourth year and the lower sixth—though we're supposed to say years nine and ten and twelve now, Helen tells me. And half the work had been done at the beginning of the year. No one else wanted to take it up when Mrs Crossley left and Miss Feather would have been leaving when she came back from maternity leave in June.' She grinned. 'Are you wondering how I know all this? Helen chatters nineteen to the dozen and I always listen. That's why we get on so well.'

Hunter grinned back at her. 'I've one more question, and since you seem a very forthright woman I won't lead up to it subtly. Have you any reason at all to believe that Helen or any of her friends has been dabbling in drugs?'

Her face darkened but not, as Hunter first thought, with anger at the implied insult to Helen. 'That's one of Miss Feather's little ventures that someone should have vetoed. A talk to the sixth-form warning them against drug abuse. Certainly they were all interested. Some of them did a long project on it in general studies this term. Not that I believe in shutting my eyes and pretending unpleasant matters don't exist, but you've got to consider all the implications of a plan before you take it on.'

Once more she was carried away by her strong feelings and had forgotten who she was talking to. 'In a better economic climate, half those sixth-formers would be out at work. Their parents send them to school to keep them occupied and off the streets. They're bored with lessons and feel they're losing face when the ones who do have academic ambitions are doing well. Lecturing on drug abuse is putting ideas into their heads and if someone's on that game then Julia Feathers must bear some responsibility for it.'

Chapter 9

As Browne walked through the precinct towards it, business at Mason's seemed much as usual. For a Tuesday morning, trade was brisk. The smashed glass had been neatly replaced and he noticed a faint smell of fresh putty as he peered into the window. Having admired the display he pushed open the door and was startled as a loud buzzing reverberated through the sales area. The shop was roughly divided in two, half kept for the dispensing of medicaments and the other half for the display and sale of toiletries that perfumed the whole. Browne hoped to be invited to wherever the smell of ground coffee had its source. The girl behind the counter laughed.

'The bell's making everybody jump. It's only been in since the weekend. Not that it's much help when the thieves come in through the window but we can only do our best.'

Mason came from the back room to cast an overseeing eye. He was small and slight with a dapper moustache and neat white coat. Browne thought Dean's description 'prissy' had been apt as the chemist came forward, communicating as effectively with his features and his hands as with his tongue. Browne had some slight acquaintance with him and submitted politely to effusive good wishes for his family.

'Soon have this business cleared up now

there's a DCI on the job.' He took Browne into the back room and poured from the jug of ready-filtered coffee simmering on an electric plate. He apparently expected to be asked exactly what stock he had lost in the robbery and he embarked on his ready-prepared answer without benefit of question. 'Two formulations of diethylpropion marketed as Tenuate and Apisate and there are a few capsules of Ponderax but that's fenfluramine—'

'Just a minute. I'm not likely to recognize that lot if I see them lying in the gutter.'

Mason rolled his eyes. 'I started to describe them to Constable Dean and he was offended. Said he could do his own homework.'

Browne sighed. Dean had the enquiry well in hand but he had evidently been spreading sweetness and light in his own inimitable manner. He grimaced at Mason. 'I'm too old to show off. Tell me what they look like and if you really want to help things along you could refill my cup with the magic brew.'

Soothed and urbane again, Mason granted both requests. 'Tenuate comes in white bevelled oblong tablets. Apisate has two yellow layers and the Ponderax

170

was in capsules with a clear body and an opaque blue cap. That might not help you, though.'

'Why not?'

'Because your punters will probably have prepared it for injection. Lemon juice or a solution of powdered citric acid is best for their purposes.'

The girl called out and Mason went to the communicating door to deal with her query.

'Who is she?' Browne demanded as Mason sat down again.

'My niece, Shirley. Good worker. Been here ever since she left school seven years ago.'

Browne nodded. Dean had not mentioned the girl but it seemed unlikely that she would suddenly have decided to abuse her position after seven years of exemplary service. 'What's the proper use of all these pills?' he asked. He saw the question had embarrassed Mason who tried to distract him with a mini-lecture.

'They're all psycho-stimulants—they increase the activity of the brain. Back in 1933 they were found to be useful for treating lung congestion. By 1946 the pharmaceutical industry had actually

171

developed a list of thirty-nine clinical uses for them, ranging from morphine addiction to persistent hiccups. They were promoted as being effective without being addictive—but then, all abused drugs had this claim made for them originally.'

It was very pat. Browne suspected that all this informatioin had been collected to impress the insufferable Dean and that his own question had merely given Mason an opportunity to give it a second airing. He decided to make a contribution. 'Amphetamines were called "pep pills", weren't they? My father tells me they were distributed to the forces in the Second World War.'

Mason nodded. 'In the 1950s everyone used them. They were even given to race horses! And so, of course, the dangers came to light and we stopped using them, but back-street chemists found plenty of customers and had no trouble supplying them. The drug's easy to make and the ingredients easy to find.'

Browne refused a third cup of excellent coffee. 'What do the customers get for their expensive fixes?' Mason looked puzzled. 'I mean what symptoms are we looking for? I know you've explained all this to Constable

Dean already but—'

'No, I haven't. He'd done that homework as well.' This time Mason was benevolent and they smiled together at the brash confidence of the young. 'I'll tell you though. A single high dose on a beginner would lead to severe headache, sweating, dry mouth, large pupils, tremor and nausea. You'd get a similar effect from a low dose and strenuous activity. Sustained low dosage leads to restlessness and an increase in physical activity. The addict repeats simple acts, polishing and repolishing shoes, throwing a ball against a wall. They talk a lot about odd topics, excitedly, and sometimes become incoherent.'

'Can I change my mind and have that third cup of coffee?'

Mason chuckled. 'If you develop all the symptoms I've described in your case it'll be caffeine poisoning. Your constable was interested in amphetamine abuse in sport.' Browne nodded. 'It's used at the trackside. Injections usually. It causes an immediate rush, makes the recipient feel capable and very confident and it delays and masks the warning symptoms of exhaustion.'

'Sounds lethal.'

'Sometimes it is.'

Another appeal from Shirley left Browne sufficient time to make notes on the information he had received and the questions it had raised in his mind. When Mason returned a second time he asked him about the shop's security system and the chemist took him on a tour of the spotless basement where most of his stock was kept. There was a window grille and the outer door was barred. Mason displayed the key which looked too complicated to be easily copied. The controlled drugs cabinet was a sturdy box of one-eighth-inch steel plate, measuring some three feet by eighteen inches by nine inches. It had double-turn locking but the thief had circumvented the lock by levering open a riveted angle with considerable force.

Browne gazed at the damage abstractedly. 'Why were these amphetamines in your cabinet if they aren't prescribed any more?'

Mason looked uncomfortable. 'I kept them at first for the very occasional prescription. It's still used short term for weight loss. Then they got past the end of their shelf life and I was always meaning to clear them out.'

'Who has keys?'

174

'I do, but occasionally I leave them with Shirley.'

'Not Michael?'

He shook his head. 'He's just the Saturday boy. I don't know him all that well. He's a neighbour of Shirley's. She told him I was looking for a part-timer.'

'Are you satisfied with him?'

Mason considered. 'I suppose he works as hard as any other teenager for what I pay.' He chuckled. 'Michael was astonished at the extent of the police enquiry. He thought there'd just be a token sprinkling of fingerprint powder once DC Dean realized we'd not lost any heroin or cocaine.'

Browne asked about the type of drugs stocked and Mason's method of ordering and filing before returning to ground level.

On the way out, ignoring the queue of customers glaring at him, Browne had a word with Shirley. One of the customers shouted 'Shop!' and Mason emerged from his retreat and resentfully began to serve. Shirley was dumpy and sallow, though she had good ankles, alert eyes and thick, shiny hair. She seemed overcome by the sight of her uncle performing her duties but admitted to being a neighbour of the Cunningham family and volunteered that she and Michael had 'knocked about together for a while'. When Browne looked surprised she flushed. 'He always seemed much older than he actually is.'

'And it was about the time you were "knocking about" that he got you to introduce him to your uncle?' She glared at him and he felt ashamed. 'How long has he worked here?' He could best spare her feelings now by getting his questions over as quickly as possible.

'Since his October half term. He came in on the Wednesday before he started to see where everything was kept and how we went about things. Uncle Jack does the prescriptions and answers the customers' questions about all the medicines. Michael was just needed to serve shaving things and hair slides to the Saturday crowds and Uncle Jack was really looking for a girl, but Michael's interested in the medical side. He asks me all sorts of things but he doesn't like asking Uncle too much.'

'And you can tell him?'

'Oh, yes. Uncle Jack thinks all women have space between their ears but I've learned most of what there is to know about dispensing since I've worked here.'

He thanked her. 'I'll let you get back to

your queue. It's not for too long now—it's your half day, isn't it?'

She shook her head. 'The shop's shutting but I'm staying on for stocktaking. We're expecting the Pharmaceutical Society inspector later in the week and we've got behind with the invoices.' She lowered her voice and looked under her eyebrows at her uncle, who was being charming to a heavily made-up lady. 'There are far too many to check. We stick them on a spike when the delivery man's gone and I'm supposed to enter them up when the shop shuts. Michael helps me on Fridays sometimes. A couple of times he's actually done it instead of me when I've been going out, but Uncle doesn't know and even so there are a whole lot to do before the man comes on Thursday morning.'

Browne commended Michael's generosity in offering this extra help, then raised his voice again in farewell. Shirley returned to her queue and Mason shook hands affably.

'Do I report any further developments to you?'

Browne shook his head. 'No, you stick with DC Dean. My enquiries are into the death of Julia Feather.'

His mouth fell open. 'The girl found at the end of the charity walk?'

Browne nodded.

'Michael's new girlfriend?' Shirley's tone echoed her employer's.

Browne looked thoughtful. 'Maybe she was.'

Browne waited for Hunter at their usual table at the Fleece. He deliberately switched his mind away from his visit to Mason's, savoured the half of best bitter in his hand and wondered how all the people who had queued in front of him at the bar managed to be free to drink on a working Tuesday. They were not snatching quick business lunches and they seemed far too well dressed and free spending to be unemployed. Even Hunter, appearing now through the swing doors, seemed by contrast merely neat and tidy. He watched as his sergeant used his height to obtain prompt service and smiled as he approached bearing his usual abstemious half. He moved over to make room on the upholstered bench.

'I had to eat out today. It was Hannah's birthday yesterday and I was foolish enough to get her the CD she wanted. Two

Shostakovitch violin concertos—dreadful racket. She's delighted and when I'm in I'm keeping my study door shut.' Hunter made no reply but buried his nose in his tankard. 'She's making dire rumblings about having it decorated that I'm resisting vigorously. What do I want it a different colour for? And who cares if the curtains stick and won't meet properly? I always enjoy watching you trying not to be irritated by them when we have one of our sessions. I shall have nowhere left to retreat to. Annette's always tidying up around us at your place and when I drop in on Benny there's nowhere to sit for packets of disposable nappies and piles of books. Ginny's taken five short months to create mayhem!'

The bottom half of Hunter's face emerged from the glass for his objection. 'That's gross exaggeration and it's a bit unfair to blame it on Virginia. There are three people living there now instead of one and there's always a bit of disorder around a baby. Personally I feel a bit more comfortable there now that it isn't so unnaturally immaculate. Considering the size of the place they do well.'

'I suppose so. I'd have thought by now

Benny would have been looking for a house.'

Hunter finished his beer and returned to Mitchell's defence. 'What's so "failed" or inhibiting about living in a flat? In Germany or America everybody does it. It's only in Britain that you haven't made it if you haven't got a stately home in its own acres. How's Virginia getting on with her course?'

'Nearly finished her second year.' Browne reached for the menu, propped against the salt and pepper pots, to indicate that it was time they returned to their two main purposes in sitting here, fuelling their energies and discussing the case. 'Hannah does sterling grandmother duties and according to Ginny it's all going well.'

He congratulated himself as he attacked his promptly served lasagne. Years of pointing out that Mitchell had many good qualities to compensate for his brashness had done nothing to alter Hunter's animosity towards him. His new policy of occasional criticisms of his son-in-law when he and Hunter were alone together had his sergeant leaping to Mitchell's defence. 'How did you get on with Helen Rowe?'

Hunter pushed a piece of lemon sole around his plate. 'You didn't give me a time limit and I thought it would be better to see her after school than to pull her out of lessons. I went to chat to her mother.' He described his conversations with Mrs Rowe. 'She told me more about the Saxbys than her own family.' Abandoning the fish, Hunter returned to the dregs of his flattish beer. 'How did it go at Mason's?'

'Want another?' When Hunter shook his head, Browne summoned the waiter, ordered coffee, then gave his sergeant an account of his morning. 'The girl, Shirley, says only Mason is supposed to sign for drugs delivered by the secure vehicle but in practice any of the three of them did it. I imagine Michael's little game will have stopped for the present, but we don't know how much of the stuff he's got stashed away. Mason was very vague about the amounts that were missing—tried to distract me by being very precise about its properties. If Michael isn't well supplied with reserves, some of his customers will suddenly be coming off the stuff. I asked Mason what would happen to someone who was using it regularly and then stopped. I'm afraid the withdrawal symptoms he described just about matched the condition you would expect to be in if, in addition to school work, play rehearsals and race meetings, you had just completed a twenty-mile walk through the night. It doesn't help us much.' The coffee arrived and Browne remarked appreciatively on its prompt delivery.

The waiter grinned. 'We get a fair bit of trade from the station. We obviously do a better job than your canteen. We'd lose it if we kept busy men waiting.'

When he was out of earshot, Hunter asked, 'You think Michael staged the break-in this week as a cover to account for the drugs that this Pharmaceutical Society inspector would find missing?'

'It seems likely. I want to know how much of the school's sporting success is drug-related, how many of the youngsters are involved. I'll have to speak to somebody, Ledgard perhaps for a start, on the feasibility of testing them. Would they be tested at race meetings? Tim's into athletics, isn't he?'

Hunter shrugged. 'Yes, when it doesn't clash with his cricket, but it's exams this summer, so he hasn't done much of either.

182

I've never seen any signs of testing when we've taken him to race meetings—not inter-school ones. He hasn't made it to county level yet. They test there, of course. Is this one for the drugs squad, or is it small scale enough to deal with it ourselves?'

'I'll get on to them. It's probably too late to raid the house, he'll have moved everything.' They drained their cups but continued to sit, Browne staring unseeing at the table top, Hunter tapping it restlessly with his forefinger nail whilst twiddling a tendril of hair with the other hand. Browne grinned at him. 'You're displaying most of the characteristics Mason described to me. It's a good job I know it's normal for you.'

Hunter stopped tapping but continued to finger his hair. 'We're considering Michael Cunningham as a very small-time dealer, but what else? Do we think that Julia Feather was on to him—or on to one of the others, and did one of them despatch her for it?'

'We've plenty of options.' Browne stood up and began to gather his belongings. 'We haven't thought about a parent protective of his child's reputation—or what about

183

Julia's bullying of Fiona Manley?'

'Or Benny's theory about Hilary Deakin?' Hunter put in.

Browne folded a note inside the bill and then made for the door. 'He seems very fond of it. I'm sure we can leave that one to his assiduous care.'

As the door closed behind them the waiter came to clear their table. He was used to these two. As usual the little dark one had eaten like a wolf and the tall fair one had just messed his food about before leaving it. Better clear it away quickly. It wasn't a very good advertisement for the pub that paid his wages.

Browne and Hunter arrived back at the office in good time for the meeting they had called for two o'clock, but the rest of the team was before them. As they filed in and found perches, Browne remarked, 'When we've given the news of Julia's death to various people they've said they were shocked and sorry but no one has seemed particularly grieved. A kind of relief seems to have been a common reaction.' He noticed that Mitchell had won the race to the most comfortable chair but then given it up to Jennie. Silence fell as he seated himself behind the desk. 'Richard rang in. He says Julia walked to church leaving her car outside the house. Metcalfe met her from church and they went off in his car. She was wearing a tartan mini-kilt and a black body.'

'What's a body?' Hunter wanted to know.

Mitchell, whose new wife was fond of that particular garment, enlightened him. 'It's an all-in-one effort, a bit like a swimsuit but the top's less revealing. You just wear a skirt over it.'

'So how would she manage...' His voice trailed away and his face was scarlet.

Browne laughed. 'You'll have to interview someone to find out, but it won't go on your action sheet. You can follow it up in your own time. Right, we know she went home to change.' He looked at Jennie. 'You were gong to ask Miss Deakin.'

Jennie nodded, then glanced at Mitchell. 'Hilary says she didn't look in Julia's room till she came back with Kit Travers. Everything then was tidily put away.' Browne indicated that she should continue. 'Her lunch wasn't a success. She met her friend in the wine bar in Station Square but they quarrelled and she walked out on him. She can't say exactly when but the table was booked for twelve forty-five and the service was quick. The quarrel got serious between the two courses. She'd been going to have a lift to school and she had to walk. It was drizzling but she was wearing a hooded coat.'

'I thought she went by car to fetch the Saxby girl.'

'Yes, in the Mini belonging to Mrs Travers.'

Browne consulted a report in his file. 'Julia was seen by a neighbour, leaving the house about one forty. She got in her car and drove down the road in the right direction for school.'

Mitchell was fidgeting, not willing to relinquish his theory. 'Why couldn't it have been Hilary in Julia's clothes? They lived together. They were both about five feet five with short straightish blonde hair. They could easily be mistaken for each other by a neighbour fifty yards or so away.'

'She'd have had to change again.'

'She'd have had plenty of time. It's about ten minutes' drive to school and she might not have known that Julia had arranged to collect Emma.'

Browne was not convinced. Apart from the lack of discernible motive, what he had heard from witnesses and seen in photographs suggested that the women were quite different types. Hilary was smart and crisp and businesslike, whilst not being unfeminine. Julia seemed to have been unconsciously provocative, a traditionally virtuous maiden but with pouting lips, thrusting hips and a bouncing bosom, modestly hidden under loose sports clothes and all the more tempting for that. 'Keep rooting,' was all he said before he moved on to other aspects.

'We've sorted out the gobbledygook on the tape. Apparently the girl playing Titania, Wendy Malik, has a grandmother living in Cloughton who speaks no English. According to Wendy, in her grandmother's generation some Asian men living in this country stopped their wives picking up English ideas of female emancipation by refusing to let them learn the language. Julia was teaching her—wouldn't she just? —and setting her a good example by learning some Urdu, just to show how easy it is to cross such cultural barriers. My informants tell me the message deals with nothing more sinister than the weather and the old lady's state of health. It was for Julia to listen to and practise. Oh, and the photographs have been picked up, collected with the chit that was in her purse.'

They passed round the twenty-four colour prints which began with a group photograph of what they supposed was the school athletics team, all looking shiny clean and smart in their matching kit. Julia's expertise with the camera had not been equal to action shots and there followed ten or a dozen blurred pictures of race winners arriving at the tape, triumphant but unrecognizable. The next two were of Julia and Andrew Metcalfe sitting outside a continental-type café eating ice-cream. Julia, in a T-shirt, looked uncomfortably cold. Two teenagers featured in the next few shots, both dressed in the uniform of Holmbrooke High School. In one they made threatening gestures towards each other, in the others they merely stood some distance apart, regarding each other, but in all of them, in spite of their mundane dress, violent ill-will crackled between them.

'Play characters, I suppose,' Jennie commented as she passed them on. There followed several pictures of a group of people relaxing in a well-kept garden, then one of Julia seated at a dinner table paying close attention to a thick-set man in evening dress. Julia was wearing the black dress now hanging in the wardrobe.

'That's Saxby,' Hunter commented when it reached him. The final picture showed Saxby and three more men similarly dressed, looking over their shoulders as they stood at a bar.

Browne collected the photographs up and replaced them in their wallet. 'At some point we'll ask Mr Saxby what the occasion was. Meanwhile we'll hear about your morning, Benny.'

'I agree with Jerry, sir, that it would be better not to interrupt the school people during the day.' He still used Hunter's forename self-consciously, Browne noted. 'I went to David Travers' surgery and he was just about to start on his rounds. He talked to me for fifteen minutes or so, then asked if I could see him later if there was any more. He did the walk with his wife and says he noted nothing amiss. They came along the canal path at about four forty. He said he wasn't Julia's GP and as far as he knew she hadn't consulted a doctor since she came to Cloughton. I don't see how he'd know. My wife's cousins don't confide their medical secrets to me.'

'He'd know where to stick a knife even better than Fiona Manley,' Jennie observed.

Mitchell glared at her, anxious to make his main point. 'Can we hear the tape again, sir? Travers' voice sounded quite familiar to me.'

Chapter 10

'I spent most of the walk,' Helen Rowe told Hunter, 'wondering whether Daniel had dropped in his tracks and fallen asleep somewhere.' She tucked her feet under her in one corner of the sofa in her mother's sitting room and granted rather than submitted to her interview. Her fair hair was pulled back on top of her head. The healthy, scrubbed-clean face stood up well to this severity, attractive because of its finely textured skin, well-arched brows and pleasant expression. She had none of

190

Emma's delicate prettiness. The afternoon had turned warm and the school uniform had been replaced by denim shorts and a T-shirt sufficiently faded for the logo on her chest to be indecipherable.

'In between,' she went on, 'we were making up silly reasons why Miss Feather missed the rehearsal and moaning about our blisters and wishing the wind would drop.'

'Tell me about the play.'

She looked surprised but obliged him. 'You know Mrs Crossley started it before Christmas?' Hunter nodded. 'When Miss Feather came she heard some of us grumbling because we'd been to rehearsals and learned some of our lines for nothing. It's a fairly stupid play. All the middle part happens because the Duke says he can't change the Athenian law and let Hermia marry the man she's in love with—and then at the end he changes his mind and tells Egeus they can all marry who they like. Doing a play isn't stupid, though. It's like being in the First Eleven in hockey, or the orchestra. You all work hard at it together and after a bit it matters more than anything and you forget that you don't like some of the other people in it. And, somehow, when it's over, you all still belong to each other.'

Hunter smiled. 'Samuel Pepys called *A Midsummer Night's Dream* "The most insipid, ridiculous play that I ever saw in my life," ' he told her.

Helen's face lit up. 'That's just what Miss Feather quoted to all the gym club boys she wanted. Canny, wasn't she? She told them a famous person had made rude remarks about it so that any objections they came up with wouldn't be anything original or different. When they said fairies were soppy she said they only would be if that was the way they played them.' Helen's manner became more confidential. 'Mrs Crossley only offered to produce the play because she liked to curry favour with the head. Miss Feather really wanted to do it.'

'And what about Mr Naylor?'

'Oh, the English department's newest member is always expected to give a hand with everything. He didn't want to do it either till Miss Feather came, then he was around at every practice, but he didn't have any ideas to suggest. I heard him saying to Miss Feather when she first took over that the play was stilted because Shakespeare's too ambitious for school children.'

'And what did she say?'

'She said that in Shakespeare's time seventeen was well grown up and that years ten and twelve were just of an age to understand the problems of crossed lovers. Then she said it was stilted because it was badly cast.'

Mrs Rowe put her head round the door but did not enter until Helen indicated that the interview was not private.

'Coffee?' They nodded their thanks and she disappeared.

'Were you in the original cast?'

Helen nodded. 'Yes, because I behave myself. Mrs Crossley left out anybody who was a bit stroppy so she ended up with a load of people who did as they were told and couldn't do much else. She had to cut out two of Titania's long speeches because Carolyn couldn't do them. Miss Feather put them back in and gave the part to Wendy. That didn't please the staff. They thought she was too loud and coarse though they found more tactful objections. Miss Feather said she was just the right type. She's big and fat and they said the costume wouldn't fit her but Miss Deakin's just finished making her another one. It's funny...' She got up as she heard her mother's footsteps and opened the door. 'Wendy isn't fat when she's on the stage and speaking her lines.' Having talked herself dry, Helen buried her face in the mug her mother handed her.

'Was Michael Cunningham in the original cast?'

She gulped and shook her head. 'No, and he didn't come to be auditioned either but Miss Feather talked him into it. She said for any credibility Titania and Oberon had to be wild spirits of today, perhaps people outside normal restraints. That appealed to Michael.'

'He's a bit wild, is he?' Having dispensed her refreshments Mrs Rowe departed without waiting for her daughter's answer. Hunter wondered if she were really so incurious as she appeared.

Helen's nose wrinkled. 'Not wild exactly. He likes having power over people, making people scared of him. He torments the life out of Mr Naylor and he torments Amanda Richards—a year nine girl who's a fairy. She's not a gymnast but she sings one of the songs. Maybe it's because he's failed all his GCSEs.' She answered Hunter's unspoken question. 'He's eighteen, a year older than the rest of year twelve. He had to repeat year eleven and do all the exams again so while his friends had moved into the sixth-form—yes, we still talk about a sixth-form—he had to stay down with us. There's quite a difference in the way the staff treat people who're doing A-levels and in what they're allowed to do. Michael lost face a lot and had to impress us.'

Hunter said, tentatively, 'I've heard a few rumours about Michael and Miss Feather...'

Helen laughed scornfully. 'If you have, he started them. Most of the immature girls have a crush on her and a few of the more sophisticated lads fancy her—enough to try to please her by doing the walk and so on.' She paused, considering. 'I don't know if it's of any interest to you but there was a silly catchphrase that Michael and some of his friends kept using. "More haste less speed." Michael kept dragging it into the conversation. He said it to Dan on Sunday afternoon and once, when he tripped up the stage steps on one of his entries, Miss Feather said it to him. It didn't go down too well. He said afterwards that she meant he was too hot for her, was rushing her. We all laughed and that went down even worse.'

'What do you remember,' he asked her, 'about the talk on drug abuse that Miss Feather arranged for you to hear?'

She was silent for some seconds, then half rose to her feet. 'I made notes. I've got them upstairs if you want to see them.'

He waved her down again, disappointed. He had not expected her to resort to deliberately misunderstanding his question. 'What sort of reaction did it get?'

'Mixed.'

'Is that all you've got to say?'

'Nobody had anything to say at the end. We were supposed to ask questions but there was one of those awful silences. Actually, it was Mr Naylor who filled it. He managed to sound really fascinated, though he wasn't talking to the man from the sports council like we all wanted to. He was asking the other one about the things he'd said about how drugs cause personality changes.

'None of us dared ask that man any questions because we hadn't understood anything he said—it had all been above our heads. It got really boring listening to the two of them talking together so in the end some of us did manage to pluck up courage to ask the sports man something just to get Mr Naylor to shut up. It was quite interesting at the end.'

As Hunter was leaving, she added, thoughtfully, 'Almost everyone in the school wanted to please Miss Feather. I don't think it was a good thing. We were too much influenced, less ourselves.'

Shaking his head, Hunter reminded himself that this girl was only seventeen!

At a first glance Michael Cunningham could have passed for twenty-five, but a looseness about his mouth and a slight hesitation in his manner as he addressed Browne, though not in the way he growled at his young brother, gave away his youth.

He despatched Paul none too politely to make a pot of tea. Paul put his pen down and closed his school books before he obliged. Michael pushed a magazine he had been reading under his armchair from where a small corner with bright lettering stuck out tantalizingly. Physically the boys were very similar, with strong features, swarthy skin, a prominent nose and a lean jaw. Both had dark hair falling just below the ears, Paul's well washed and tidy, Michael's lank, in greasy clumps. Browne knew the difference was as likely to be caused by his age and hormones as by a lack of hygiene. The important differences between them lay in Michael's hunched shoulders, his scowl and his aggressive manner.

He abandoned the latter for an overdone nonchalance when Browne's questions began. His fellow sixth-formers were dismissed as 'childish', the school staff, 'power-happy, big fishes in a little pool'. Julia's death was a 'great loss' in mock funeral tones. Browne clenched his fists in his pockets and asked about Michael's duties at Mason's.

'I sell cheap cosmetics to girls who wouldn't be beautiful if they spent a fortune.'

'What about Friday nights?'

'That's not official. The old git leaves her to do the invoices and sometimes expects her to sweep up as well. If I'm passing I give a hand. After all, I got the job through her.'

Browne met Paul's glance as he carried in the tea tray. 'Doesn't sound much like the Michael we all know and love, does it? What can you tell me about the break-in?'

Michael shrugged. 'See your constable's report—if you can read his scribble.' Deliberately, Browne took his cup from Paul, sat down and drank his tea before continuing. 'How did you hear about Miss Feather's death?'

Michael disposed of half his own tea before replying, 'My little fan, Emma, told me someone had stuck the knife in.'

'Is that exactly what she told you?'

'You make the point sound important.'

Browne's patience snapped. 'Not really. I just don't want you inconvenienced by having to walk past any more bodies.' He saw Michael's grin of triumph at this deviation from protocol and took a hold on himself. 'What exactly did Emma say?'

He shook his head. 'I can't remember.'

'Did she mention a knife?'

He was on his guard now. 'She must have done or how would I know?'

'And who did you pass the news on to?'

'No one. It sounded so fantastic I thought I'd better ring up and check.'

'You had no qualms about ringing a member of staff's private number?'

He strolled across the room before turning and smiling. 'Not that one.'

As Michael stood in front of the fireplace, Browne moved to the armchair he had been occupying, sliding it backwards as he seated himself and revealing the magazine, *Man of Steel.* Yellow capitals offered, 'BASIC BRAWN—the Super 10 size Regimen' and red ones, 'Intensity! UP YOURS WITH MR OLYMPIA'S HELP.' Between the two, a black man with muscles that bulged monstrously held aloft a bar with what seemed an unlikely collection of weights.

Browne smiled. 'The drugs squad tell me these publications have half-page advertisements for underground books that are very explicit. I see you've marked one.' He riffled through the pages. 'Sent for this, have you?'

Encouraged by the flash of alarm on Michael's face, he went on, 'Do you mind if I have a look round your room, Michael?' The boy moved his shoulders, evidently not minding as much as Browne had hoped. 'And yours, Paul. Mustn't show any favouritism.'

Michael sprang forward. 'That's different. Paul's under age. My parents are out.'

But Paul seemed anxious to prove his innocence of whatever crime was being investigated. 'I don't mind. If they wait for Mum and Dad to be in it'll be a long wait.'

Michael glowered without speaking as Browne went to the window and signalled to the three men in the car on the opposite side of the road. The DCI and the two boys sat silent as they took the house apart. They had found nothing an hour later when the Cunningham parents returned.

When he came to take his briefing on Wednesday morning, Browne had still not forgiven himself for so badly misjudging his confrontation with the Cunninghams. He described the fracas ruefully. 'I should have started the search before I asked any questions. Nothing was found on the boys and Paul refused to admit to having removed anything from his bedroom. Cunningham Senior took five minutes to run out of reprisals to threaten me with.'

Mitchell, who would certainly have kicked the door in first and asked permission afterwards, on this occasion had the good sense not to say so. Instead, he gave a brief summary of his unfruitful session with an assortment of footsore youngsters before giving way to Jennie.

She had been similarly employed and had little to add.

Browne made ticks on his list and turned to his next point. 'We've had no reported sightings of the car. Keep asking. I want to know everywhere it went between the house and the Red Lion. As we expected, forensic has found hairs and fibres of every conceivable type and colour. There were a couple of long dark hairs on the back of the driving seat, though. Ask if anyone but Julia is known to have driven it. What did you get from Helen Rowe, Jerry?'

Hunter grinned. 'The shrewdness and wisdom I'd expect from someone much older, and sensible to boot. She made some pretty knowing comments on the people we're interested in but she wasn't offering many hard facts. She's the sort of girl I think the others might confide in—and she has a co-operative mother.'

'You're saying it's worth having another go at her?'

Hunter nodded. 'The soft approach, though. I don't think there's any chance of frightening her into being disloyal.'

Another tick went on Browne's list. 'According to all the marshals, only two wheelchairs passed over the course, both occupied by disabled participants. I've had someone working on Julia's diary. There were a lot of initials with phone numbers in the back. They've all been rung without much joy, but one of them was Derek Saxby. He did a lot of spluttering and said it was also his wife's and daughter's number. Julia would hardly have filed it under his initials if she'd wanted to ring them but we let it go for the time being.'

'There's the photograph as well.'

'So there is, Benny. We'll take it and show it to him and ask him about the phone number face to face. Perhaps Richard would have the right touch if he can fit it in.' Browne smiled grimly. 'Let's see what we can dig up about Saxby's spare-time interests. I'm in court for the rest of the day, so no afternoon session in my office. I think the best use of the time for the rest of you will be to rattle through another score or two of those walkers before they've completely forgotten that they took part, never mind noticed anything. Yes, Jerry?'

'That's fine up to about half past three, but Helen was telling me the plans for the play. Mrs Travers is taking over since the production is so well on. There's to be a run-through of the whole play after school tonight so that she can get the feel of it and judge what's still needed. Are Benny and I still to go?'

Browne winked at him. 'Oh yes, no reprieve.'

Chapter 11

To Hunter's enormous relief, as their car left the station and set out for the school, Mitchell announced, 'I had to do this play for O-level at Heath Lees.' Now he would not have to explain its fanciful complexities to his scornful and philistine passenger.

Assuming Hunter's ignorance, Mitchell did the explaining himself. 'It starts with a pair of royals moaning because they can't hurry time and so they have to wait for their wedding day like everyone else. Then, there's a pair of eloping lovers who are daft enough to tell her girl friend where they're off to, and she goes trailing after them. Then there's a group of what our teacher called rude mechanicals. That made us hopeful for a while, but they weren't rude at all, just stupid and out to make a quick buck from entertaining the royal lot after the wedding. Then there's a crowd of crazy spirits making mischief amongst the humans and the whole shoot end up in the same wood! I gave up trying to keep track after that, O-level or no O-level.'

'Did you pass?'

Mitchell chuckled. 'Believe it or not, yes. He was some teacher. Are we giving the school a reason for our turning up at this practice?'

Hunter shook his head. 'I think we'll just appear and justify our presence only if someone requires us to. Better let the head know that we're in school, though.'

Eventually, they found the school hall by following a gaggle of excited children, went in and stood at the back. Helen Rowe noticed them, beamed, brought her teacher across and introduced them all. Hunter scrutinized Kit Travers. She was tall and rangy, fair and smartly dressed, with an air of authority.

Mitchell nodded towards Helen. 'Nice manners.' There was no irony in his voice. Obviously the girl had made the same impression on Mitchell as on himself. Mrs Travers greeted them but made no comment on their arrival and the children, under her eagle eye, took no notice of them but made last-minute adjustments to their costumes or took up their positions to begin.

'The staff look so young and the sixth-formers so sophisticated, I'm not sure which are which,' Hunter offered.

'None of the masters is in doublet and hose,' Mrs Travers informed him, solemnly, before moving off to direct operations. Naylor hovered irritatingly behind her.

'That English master,' Mitchell muttered, 'looks more wet behind the ears than most of the actors.'

Ignoring him, Kit Travers signalled to the fairies to begin their mime. She liked Julia's version of the first scene even better on this second viewing. When Egeus entered, she was sharply reminded of Derek Saxby. The Duke Theseus greeted him affably, but immediately he began his tirade.

'Full of vexation come I, with complaint
Against my child, my daughter Hermia.'

Andrew, in his part, was behaving exactly as Saxby did at parents' evenings, returning a cheerful greeting with a diatribe against Emma's teachers and friends. Basically, Saxby wanted what Egeus was demanding.

'I beg the ancient privilege of Athens
As she is mine, I may dispose of her.'

Hermia's line, a few moments later, was uttered with heartfelt conviction. 'I would my father looked but with my eyes.' The absence of any scenery showed her the real drama in Emma's performance. She was Hermia, wondering at herself as she besought the Duke's support. 'I know not by what power I am made bold.' Emma knew the courage it needed to defy a violent man.

The two lovers, one the father's choice, the other the daughter's, pleaded their causes before the prince. The conflict in the scene was between father and child and Shakespeare had made the young men colourless. James Bennett, playing Demetrius, was just that, but Daniel Stevens was making a personable and flamboyant Lysander.

'I am, my lord, as well deriv'd as he,
As well posess'd: my love is more than
    his:
My fortunes every way as fairly rank'd'

He compelled sympathy, crackled with
vitality. The silly scene borrowed a significance from the personalities of these
children Julia had chosen and worked on.
She was a witch.

She must have been to have bewitched
Dave. How long, Kit wondered, had her
husband resisted? And what outcome had
Julia envisaged? Surely a serious affiliation
with the Roman Catholic church precluded
a cheap fling and she could hardly envisage
marriage to a divorced man. Kit shook her
head. Dave, that most uxorious of men,
considering divorce? Yet, what else was she
to think?

Complaining to her about the amount
Julia used their joint telephone, Hilary had
produced their itemized bill, with long calls
to their own number systematically logged.
She herself saw Julia at school five days
a week and had never, as far as she
could remember, spoken to her on the
telephone.

And then, twice, she had seen them together, once in a coffee bar and then coming out of the Last Straw at the sleazy end of town. All of this might have added up to nothing, if only, when she'd challenged him at the summit of Stainwood Pike on Monday afternoon, he'd laughed it off. But, covered with confusion, he'd refused to explain.

She was recalled to her immediate surroundings by Helena's entry on stage. When the parents and friends in the audience who knew the everyday Helen Rowe heard the petulant and uncharacteristic whine in which she began to speak, their laughter might dissipate the cleverly built up atmosphere. It amused her now and she had seen it before. This particular talent would be wasted, she thought. Helen Rowe would want to do something of more practical use to the world than become an actress.

Towards the end of this first scene, the school secretary had crept into the hall to call Mitchell to the telephone. He returned in less than a minute, trying to keep the relief out of his face. She grinned as she heard his whisper to his colleague. 'Sorry, got to go. Gaffer wants me to help Richard out.' Hunter had smiled and seemed quite happy to let him go.

As the first scene finished, the curtains closed momentarily. Kit knew that the lower sixth-form stage hands would be sliding the forest flats across the back of the stage and willed them to finish before Adrian arrived there to 'help'. The absence of scenery meant that the switch to the workmen in the forest could be almost immediate.

The curtains drew back to reveal them preparing the entertainment that they hoped would make their fortunes when they produced it at the royal wedding. 'I think Prince Charles would have appreciated such an initiative at his own ceremony,' she whispered to Hilary, who had come to sit beside her. The Athenian workmen waited tolerantly for Naylor's head to stop peering round the flat, then swung into their lines.

She noticed that Peter Quince was played by a particularly well-spoken youth. She supposed Julia had wanted to use his slightly authoritative air as he organized his fellows and he remembered most of the time to adopt the Yorkshire dialect that came naturally to the children playing the rest of the workmen. She could see he did it with conscious mockery but doubted whether many of the audience would notice.

This scene, too, commanded admiration. The slapstick humour was controlled and the yokels' anxiety to produce an impressive performance came over to her.

There followed the scene between Puck and the fairy played by Amanda Richards. Since all the fairies were athletic rather than dainty, her ample curves were not out of place and she sang sweetly, unaccompanied,

'Over hill, over dale,
Thorough bush, thorough briar...'

Kit had learned, to her astonishment that afternoon, that the music of the songs was the original work of the music master, Phil Brooke. When and how had Julia charmed him from the exclusive work of his own department, in which, as the staff sarcastically remarked, he would 'brook no interference' and from which he could spare no time to be involved in the activities of any other?

Now, Paul Cunningham strutted up to

211

the footlights, admitting his identity to his fairy admirer. 'I am that merry wanderer of the night.' He was a nice boy, quite different from that sly and sullen brother in year twelve. Suddenly, Michael appeared from the wings. Paul's involuntary start of fear seemed genuine, Amanda's more so.

'Ill met by moonlight, proud Titania.'

Michael, as Oberon, ignored them and strode across the stage towards his queen who had entered from the other side. Kit was startled. Fat Wendy—in Hilary's cleverly designed leaf dress and her fairy character—was a new creature. She, at least, was not afraid of Michael, and flung at him accusations of unfaithfulness and misconduct with the Duke's bride-to-be. Oberon made counter-accusations.
Wendy defended herself, embarking with passion on the speech that covered a page and a half of the edition they were using and that Mrs Crossley had blue-pencilled even before the first read-through. Kit was held spellbound, from 'These are the forgeries of jealously,' right through to,

'And this same progeny of evils comes

From our debate, from our dissension;
We are their parents and original.'

Why had it needed Julia to see this girl's potential? Michael cowered a little under the torrent of words, partly in obedience to Julia's stage direction and, in some measure, in a natural reaction to the force of Wendy's personality.

Then Kit overheard Helen's whisper. 'Those two need the marriage guidance council,' and she smiled, the spell broken for her. The gestures Michael was now making towards his queen were not quite suitable for a school production. It was a good job the queen was Wendy. Michael wouldn't be having her behind the bike sheds afterwards—at least, not unless Wendy had made the suggestion herself.

Daniel Stevens had been watching the scenes that followed his own from a chair in the well of the hall. As Oberon began to explain the revenge he intended to take on Titania, he got up and took his place in the wings ready for his next entry. He preferred being on the stage to sitting and thinking.

He despised the character he was playing. Why did Lysander want to marry Hermia? She was only half a person, afraid to claim her rights. He'd heard all that Miss Feather had had to say about not thinking of act one in terms of women's lib, but, if he'd really been Lysander, he'd have given up on Hermia long ago.

Emma wasn't so different from the character she was playing. She was a good deal better looking than Helen but he could never fancy her. Not that Helen wasn't attractive, but Emma would be something really special if only she had a bit of spark about her. Helen knew who she was, though, and what she wanted and it was his good luck that that included him.

He heard Amanda begin the second verse of the spotted snakes song. Just Michael's speech now and then he was on.

'What thou see'st when thou dost wake,
Do it for thy true love take.'

Would Helen still want him if she knew what he had done?

'Wake when some vile thing is near.'

Michael laughed unpleasantly and tip-toed off stage towards him in the wings. 'Source of supply dried up for the moment,' he remarked out of the side of his mouth. 'Might put the price up a bit. Still, I'm sure you'll manage it.'

He brushed past and made way for Emma to take Daniel's arm and lean on him as they stumbled on to the stage.

'Fair love, you faint with wand'ring in the wood,
And, to speak troth, I have forgot our way.
We'll rest us, Hermia.'

He sank with Emma to the wooden stage floor, as tremulous and disorientated as the dolt he was playing. Was Michael going to start asking for payment in money? Automatically, he spoke the lines in which he argued with Hermia and was banished to sleep on the other side of the stage. When Paul came on, back right, he would have a page of dialogue in which he could lie and think.

He hadn't any money. Come to that, he hadn't much of anything any more, no real identity, no self-respect. His classmates thought he was a brilliant and dedicated athlete. Helen thought he was a good friend, someone whose company she enjoyed—maybe even a little more than that. Michael thought he was a pawn to be manipulated, a steward to attend him on his ego-trip.

In reality he was a sordid little cheat—a criminal. It couldn't go on but it mustn't all blow up whilst his mother was still alive. He must spare her that and anything he had done or had to do to prevent it was justified, at least in his own mind. This was no time to think it all out. Helen was standing over him. 'Lysander, if you live, good sir, awake.' He was being about as true to himself in his running as Helen was to herself in this silly role.

He gave his answering line. 'And run through fire I will, for thy sweet sake.' Soon, he would have to. He would break with the pills and injections, break with Michael and take the consequences. Would it also mean breaking with Helen?

He leapt up and began his pursuit of her across the boards and in and out of the wings. It was ironic. In this play he was acting out his own folly, chasing after the wrong goal under the influence of drugs, offered, in both cases, by Michael. In the play, he was attacked in his sleep and had no choice. In the shower room at that Couriers' meeting, nearly six months ago now, his decision had been deliberate.

Had it really all been for his mother? Hadn't he enjoyed the glory of it for himself? He'd known then what would happen to her. His parents had never spared him by lying to him. He'd been horrified at the inevitability. There was nothing anyone could do, his father had said. He'd got just six months or so to make her proud of him.

Her father had been a runner. His county trophies were ranged on the sideboard, a witness to her pride in his success. His own prizes were a hollow offering. He suddenly made his decision. As from right now, the drugs had stopped. He closed his eyes and prayed, to any deity that might exist, for time to win just one race under his own steam before his mother died.

He suddenly found himself in the wings again, whilst Emma, lying front left by the footlights, called out for him in fear. Presumably he had spoken his lines and made the appropriate gestures since no one was looking at him. The Athenian workmen were cavorting again now. He felt no interest whatsoever in the proceedings, wished he had no part in the play, wished he had never met Helen so that he would not now have to endure her contempt.

'But hark, a voice! Stay thou but here awhile,
And by and by I will to thee appear.'

With various nods and winks, Bottom the weaver crept behind the cardboard bush into the wings and fell over Daniel's feet. He hissed at him crossly. 'Wake up, Stevens! Move yourself!' Daniel blinked, apologized and passed him the ass's head, the pride of the art department, helping the boy to slip it over his head.

When the scene drew to its close, Mrs Travers clapped her hands. 'This won't necessarily be the official interval for the performances but you've all earned a break. There's lemonade on the table at the back. Only Miss Deakin will pour it—I don't want a single drop on anyone's costume!'

Released from the spell of the poetry and the necessity to do justice to Miss Feather's production in front of the staff who were seeing it for the first time, the cast remembered their various blisters and sprains and limped from the stage for their refreshments.

Hilary Deakin, against her better judgement, had produced shortbread biscuits and she watched vigilantly for the wiping of greasy fingers on the muslins and silks and velvets she had fashioned with such pains. Hunter looked around him, then turned to her and thanked her for his lemonade. 'Are all the girls in this play beautiful?'

She grinned. 'No, but most of them are seventeen and in the top band. They have the advantages of dewy freshness and intelligence.' She handed over his allocation of two finger biscuits and he circulated around the hall, joining no particular group but listening to each in turn.

'A school play always breaks up previous romances and begins new affairs, based on proximity and shared fun.' That had to be Mrs Travers. Hunter wondered what

219

Naylor, to whom the remark was addressed, made of it. 'Of course, Helen and Daniel came in as a pair. Daniel usually knows when he's well off!'

'I thought Emma and Michael were drifting together,' Philip Brooke put in, 'but, just as I was getting worried, Emma saw the light and backed off.' He looked about at the representatives of the games, English and art departments who, with himself, had all rallied round for this resumption of Julia's play. 'Bloody woman's even bossing us about from the grave,' he observed. No one gasped. The tone was amused, even affectionate, and, whatever their motive in turning up after lessons tonight, the magic of the production was weaving its spell. Excitement was mounting.

'I think Julia was a brilliant teacher,' Adrian Naylor announced suddenly and aggressively, as though someone had made an observation to the contrary. 'The kids come from breakfast-time family quarrels, have a crowded bus journey, go to a boring assembly, there are workmen banging along the corridor, someone from the office interrupts to ask questions about dinner money. Julia could cut through all that and actually keep them busy and interested.'

The little lecture was greeted with silence. Julia's achievement was unquestioned, but it was remarkable chiefly to this teacher ill-equipped temperamentally to do the job himself.

Hunter wriggled his way unobtrusively into the group of staff. 'You don't mingle in with the cast when you take a break?'

Kit Travers answered him. 'Sometimes we do, but we have to be a bit careful, especially when they're particularly enthusiastic and excited because then they treat us like they treat each other. It has drawbacks.'

'How?'

She paused to work it out. 'Well, in a relaxed atmosphere it's very easy for both sides to say things that are unwise. Then, in formal classroom surroundings, when we're authority figures again, they remember what they've told us, regret it and, unfairly but understandably, blame us, consider we've been prying, so we don't go and join huddles of them. On the other hand, of course, we keep our ears open for the things they might say that we really should know—just as you are doing!'

Chapter 12

Browne gave his sergeant the first slot at Thursday morning's briefing. Hunter felt that the time he had spent at the rehearsal had been valuable. He had gained some insight into the staff's and the children's relationships as well as enjoying the play tremendously. He'd thought it the best school production he'd ever seen.

He could think of little, however, in the way of reportable information that he'd picked up and no words that would convey to Dean or Mitchell the advantage he felt he had gained. He mentioned Puck's flinching each time Oberon grasped him, and Helen's terse comment, 'Miss Feather seized on that but she didn't suggest it.' Oberon had cuffed all the fairies as they passed him and Hunter suspected that many of them had gone home nursing cruel nips and bruises.

One matter he had clarified as far as it was possible. 'I traced the Monday morning telephone messages. Neil Stevens told Daniel only that Julia had been found dead. Daniel says he repeated that to Helen but added that he thought we suspected murder because of "all the fuss and the number of official folk who were sent for". Helen changed nothing, just passed to Emma both Daniel's news and his opinion. Emma says she did the same but Michael claims she mentioned a knife. He may simply be trying to justify having talked about that himself when he rang Hilary Deakin's house or maybe he enjoyed trying to get Emma into trouble. He certainly got her upset.'

'He might possibly be telling the truth.'

Hunter shrugged. 'I suppose so. Oh, Mrs Travers says she lent her car to Miss Deakin rather than fetching Emma herself because Julia had more villains in the cast than Hilary could deal with on her own—or worse, with Naylor to be played off against her.

'We've not actually put any definite theory about this murder into words yet. Are we assuming that Julia found out somehow that Michael was pushing drugs, even though it was in a small way, and he killed her to shut her up.'

'We've heard enough to know there

wouldn't be any other way to shut her up.'

'You're giving us ideas, Benny.' Mitchell accepted Browne's mild reprimand and let him answer Hunter.

'We're following him up very seriously. Dean's having him watched at all times to nail the drugs business on to him but he'll let us know of anything else he turns up, naturally. Michael was in school in good time for the rehearsal.'

'Did he come in the car with his brother?'

Browne shook his head. 'No. Paul played football on Sunday morning, then ate at an Indian curry place with four or five friends. Michael says he watched television and he seemed to know all the details of what was on.'

He consulted Dean's notes again. 'After the rehearsal he dropped Emma and Helen off near their homes and then went to bed—or so he says. He turned up for the dancing and the walk. Several girls complained about him at the disco. He set out walking with James Bennett, another of the thespians, but James didn't want to fool around and he soon went on ahead. Michael hung about annoying some of

224

the girls. He was reported to two lots of marshals before he dropped out after the second check-point which was near his home. Later on he drove to the YMCA to socialize with the finishers.'

Jennie asked. 'Could he have driven the body to the far end of the track?'

Browne considered. 'It does run close to the main road but no one was seen walking in the wrong direction with a sizeable burden, and if he'd come the other way he'd have walked past Stevens and Jack Nicholls. They knew he was trouble and wouldn't have missed seeing him. Benny?'

'Is there any other way he could have dumped the body where it was found, except using the canal path?'

'He'd hardly have come across the water and the other side of the path is a very steep grassy slope up to the Rocks. There's no path down and the grass is very rough. The SOCO say there were no signs that anyone had been climbing down. I don't think the body was thrown over. The clothes were snagged and smeared but the face was completely unmarked. I think we have to conclude that she was dumped after dark but before the marshals arrived, which doesn't help us much. Everybody claims to have crept off to bed. Right, who's next?'

No one offered. The rest of the team had spent a tedious day talking to young people anxious to help them but with nothing very relevant to tell.

'All right, let's have a detailed look at the people we're interested in. Michael was at school soon after two but Julia was last seen leaving home at one forty and he was alone then. The car journey to school only takes five minutes or so. He says he was at home and asleep between dusk and the beginning of the disco. We think Julia knew or suspected he was pushing drugs he'd lifted from his place of work. What about Daniel Stevens?'

They turned to Mitchell. 'He had lunch at the hospice on Sunday with his parents. His father drove home, dropping Daniel at Green Royd branch library at about ten to two. That's about ten minutes' walk from school.

'He wouldn't have had much leeway there but there was plenty of opportunity that night. Neil Stevens was helping at the YMCA for a while before he drove out to the canal. He left the boy in bed.

Daniel gave the disco a miss. Twenty miles' hard running's plenty of exercise without dancing as well. His motive would be similar to Michael's if we're right about his being on speed.'

'Anyone else at the school a likely candidate?'

They shook their heads. 'Plenty of opportunity,' Jennie observed, 'but not much motive.'

'What about Kit Travers?'

Browne frowned at Hunter. 'She got Julia the job and brought her to Cloughton in the first place.'

'Maybe she wished she hadn't—or, what if that's what she got her here for?'

'We've no evidence for thinking that.'

'Well, Naylor, then?' Mitchell suggested.

Those who had met him at close quarters sniggered, till Jennie offered, tentatively, 'His motive could have been to protect Fiona—though he thought Julia was helping her and she thought he was half in love with Julia.'

'Fiona herself, then?'

Jennie shook her head. 'Provided we accept her handicap, it's her alibi.'

'Do we?'

Jennie nodded. 'I think so. She's missing

227

out on too much to be using it as an excuse. For the book, she was in Naylor's flat while the rehearsal was going on. She tried to stop him going and he was late back because he took home the people Julia had promised lifts to. Then Fiona went to Evensong at Dicky Birds.'

'What?' Browne interrupted, rudely.

Mitchell explained. 'Two little dicky birds, sitting on a wall, one called Peter, one called Paul...'

Browne sniffed. 'Sorry I asked. Go on, Jennie.'

'Well, eventually he turned up to meet her. They went home and to bed together till it was time for their abortive attempt to complete two hundred yards. It was only a few more hundred yards to Naylor's house but one of the walk chiefs justified his existence by delivering her. Naylor says he and Fiona spent the rest of the night together.'

There was a tap at the door and Dean came in and took the narrow space on top of Browne's table that Mitchell made for him.

'And your favourite candidate, Benny?'

'Hilary Deakin? Well, she left her boyfriend in time to have got to the

228

house. She claims she walked to school but she could have nipped back and killed Julia. Then she could have put on her clothes, driven off in her car, dumped it at the Red Lion near the school and walked from there. She has no alibi for the evening. She decided to have a night in with her feet up, adding a few stitchers to a crinoline or two.' He grinned. 'She probably planned a night of passion with the punter she fell out with earlier so she was at a loose end.

'She could easily have done it but she has no more motive than any of the others. Only Michael and possibly young Stevens had anything to gain.'

Hunter, as was his wont, had paced round Browne's office whilst the others were expounding, fiddling with Browne's possessions but thinking hard about what was being said. Now he stopped at the window and turned. 'People don't commit murder for credible, logical reasons. Remember that chap who killed any girls who used the same colloquial expression as his awful mother? What about Saxby. His picture was on the film in Julia's camera and his phone number was in her diary. Where was he on Sunday afternoon?'

Browne shook his head. 'Fairly certainly in Amsterdam but I agree that's something to get to work on. We rather wanted to see how you got on with Saxby, Richard. We'll keep a tail on Cunningham for you if you'll give him your inimitable treatment. We've nattered a bit too long now, so let's get moving.'

He reached for the action sheets, already filled in except for Dean's, rectified that omission and handed them round. 'Jerry, didn't you say the Saxby girl had some relation who stood up for her?'

Hunter nodded. 'It's Saxby's sister.'

'Splendid. Go and see if she'll reveal all about her brother. Keep using Julia's name and see what vibes you get and pick up anything else she offers. Paper work for me. I shall keep at it until I can see the surface of my desk again.' He watched the awful truth dawn on Jennie's and Mitchell's faces. 'Yes, I'm afraid it's back to the walkers for you two.'

Jennie grinned at Mitchell as they trailed up the corridor. 'You never know. We might speak this afternoon to the one walker who saw it all.' Mitchell's answer was a discourteous growl and Jennie shrugged and gave up on him. Let him sulk. She rolled her eyes at one of the dog handlers who came round the corner and received the benefit of Mitchell's glower.

The glower was not unobservant. 'Borrowed one of Hunter's shirts, Colin?'

Colin looked rueful. 'It's my brother's actually. Is it so obvious?' Gingerly he turned back the cuff of an over-long sleeve to reveal swathes of bandages. 'It's covering these. My new dog's a bit enthusiastic. I'm in court this morning, testifying against a defendant who says Rebel attacked him viciously. I'm supposed to be giving the brute a character reference. His name doesn't help.'

Mitchell was much amused. 'Better than Exterminator!' He went on his way, his good humour quite restored by his own wit.

Dean had been pleased to be considered the force's frightener. He was always glad to be sent to put pressure on people who thought they owned the whole of mankind along with their palatial houses. This one had a drive like a country lane. He hadn't been able to see the house from the gates that opened on to the street and it was not disappointing when it appeared. Dean decided he would take more care of it if it was his and tutted at the ragged lawns and flaking paint. When he was invited in he was repelled by the amateurish decoration, the chill and lack of comfort.

He had tried to find Saxby at the local branch of the computer firm of which he was managing director. They had told him Saxby often worked from home and was doing so today. Saxby enlarged on the theme. 'It's no good talking about the advantages of the goods if you don't demonstrate them. From here I'm in touch with the whole—'

Having Browne's tacit permission to annoy this witness rather took the edge off Dean's pleasure in interrupting him in mid-sentence. 'I haven't come for the sales talk. I want to know exactly what your relationship was with Julia Feather.' He was looking forward to the battle and was disappointed when Saxby took this opening shot calmly.

'I see you don't mince your words. Sorry if it doesn't suit you but I have no relationship whatsoever with—'

'We have photographs.' Saxby stared blankly. 'Perhaps you'd like to think again why your phone number is in Julia's diary.'

'I never reconsider.' Dean believed him.
'As I told your colleague, Miss Feather was
my daughter's A-level English teacher and
I may well have had cause to ring her
about—'

'Do you call her Miss Feather when
you're gazing into each other's eyes, all
dressed up in your best party clothes?'
Dean produced a copy of the photograph
but Saxby scorned to look at it.

'I don't like your tone, young man. I
shall ring—'

'The Super? He'll know what you mean.
He doesn't like it either.' Dean knew he
was pushing his luck. He realized, too, that
Saxby was more annoyed at having his own
rhetoric interrupted than by the rudeness.
He'd confine his baiting to interruptions.
'The photograph, sir.'

'Miss Feather just happened to be at the
same dinner—'

'She sat at your table. Was she your
guest?'

'As a matter of fact, yes. She was—'

'But you had no relationship whatsoever
with her?'

Saxby's lips were white but Dean thought
it was fury rather than fear. 'We were
on the same charity committees. We

didn't need a relationship for that. She probably had her picture taken with most of the men present. She was that sort of woman.'

'Go on.' But now he was allowed, he chose not to. He shrugged. 'We were just... We just met...' The explanation petered out into silence. Dean let it last ten seconds, then favoured Saxby with his most charming smile.

'Would you ask your daughter to come down to the station after school, sir? We shan't keep her long and we'll make sure she's brought safely home.'

'Dammit, man! Leave Emma out of this!' Now he was shouting. 'What do you want from her that I can't tell you?'

'I want to know why she dropped out of athletics a few weeks ago.'

Saxby had himself in hand again. He settled into his armchair and crossed his legs to demonstrate how relaxed he was. 'I don't see what connection it would have with your enquiries but I can tell you that. I told her that she must choose between her running and being in the play. Doing both would certainly interfere with her work. She chose the play because next year she'll be in the upper sixth and not allowed to audition. Did you need her for anything else?'

'Not that you could help with, I'm afraid.'

He smiled thinly. 'You couldn't see her today in any case. She's gone to Manchester with her friends, Helen and Wendy. The university has organized a day's exhibition for sixth-formers who are considering applying to do their drama course. She tells me the people from the Exchange Theatre will be there. My sister has kindly provided their transport. She spoils Emma dreadfully—but they won't be back till quite late. Is it just Emma you're persecuting or are the other two children to be subjected to your catechism?'

'You'll have to ask my CI, sir.' Dean took his leave, well pleased with this preliminary skirmish.

As soon as his car had disappeared round the bend in the drive, Saxby picked up the telephone.

As soon as Dean reached the main road he stopped the car, got out his radio and spoke to Hunter.

'I'm sorry to interrupt. I can see you're busy.' Hunter's more courteous approach to his witness met with friendliness and an offer of tea. Laura Saxby cleared away a complicated-looking collection of receipts and account books as she asked, 'Is it about Emma's teacher? Such a hard-working and enthusiastic young woman. Emma's very upset...' The torrent of words went on until the table was tidy. Hunter had the impression that Miss Saxby did not usually gush like this. She went off to brew the tea and came back calm again, bearing a pot of Darjeeling and a Madeira cake.

'What did you mean when you said Emma could do without the upset just now?'

Miss Saxby looked nonplussed. 'Well, the girl was attached to Miss Feather and she's at an awkward age.' Her manner became confiding. 'My brother's a well-meaning man but not easy for Emma—or Clare—to live with, and she's got her A-levels to worry about.'

'I've heard she's quite a clever girl who's taking the work in her stride.'

Miss Saxby nodded and cut Hunter a piece of cake. 'I'm sure you're right.'

Hunter, who seldom ate cake, toyed with it. 'I understood that you were spending the day in Manchester yourself.'

'That's right. I should have been meeting a friend who couldn't make it at the last minute. I didn't want the youngsters to feel uncomfortable so I didn't tell them. I had work to do here and it's only an hour's drive so I came back.'

She seemed, Hunter thought, not exactly resentful of his questions but embarrassed by her own answers. To his surprise she relaxed more when he asked about Julia and her brother. 'Derek does have an eye for a pretty girl. Doubtless he'd make the most of a social occasion when he could spend time with one innocently in the course of his charitable activities—but in their own peculiar way he and Clare are fond of each other. I'm sure he wouldn't jeopardize his marriage. There's never been a whisper in the past of that kind of thing.'

She began to clear the tea things without offering Hunter a second cup. 'He used to be a more affable father. He tends to take his worries about the recession out on his women and he always was a bit high-handed.'

Hunter took the loaded tray from her and carried it to the kitchen, then she returned to the dining room with him and to the subject of her niece. 'Adolescence is always difficult and when you're reproached for being an individual and for developing your own interests and personality, it's more so.'

Hunter feared a lecture from a devotee of psychology. He could think of no other way in which Laura Saxby would be involved in the case and so took his leave. He had deliberately omitted to ask why, when she was supposed to be in Manchester with Emma and Wendy, he had caught a fleeting but unmistakable glimpse of Helen Rowe at Laura Saxby's bedroom window as he had walked up the path.

When he could bear to pore over his hated files and lists no longer, Browne walked briskly along the corridor and up the stairs to the Superintendent's office. A session with Petty was hardly light relief but it was a change of occupation, getting there stretched his legs, and, in any case, it could not be put off indefinitely.

He described the various present occupations of the men assigned to his case, elaborated on the connection with Dean's investigation and gave a summary of the current state of affairs. 'And your own morning?'

Browne could never gauge Petty's mood from his questions and remarks. 'I spent it trying to see the people we're dealing with in the round. We only see people as they relate to the case, not the whole person.'

It had not been the right answer and he knew he was only getting deeper into the mire as he tried to explain. 'During the Second World War my father was sent from Sheffield to work in a factory in Manchester making planes and tanks. Occasionally, the rest of us visited him in his digs there. Madge, his landlady eked out her boarding house income by doing home dressmaking. For years afterwards it fashioned my idea of Mancunian women. I thought they all lived in the kitchen, from which they rushed every time they had a spare minute to the sewing machine, kept in a back room that was forever draped in swathes of material.

'If I'm not careful, I'll make the same mistake in this case. I'll see our suspects now only in relation to Julia Feather and what's happening to her and the reason for what happened might be something we shall only hear about when we're discussing some other aspect of their existences.'

'Like what?'

'I shan't know till I find it.'

Petty sat down heavily. 'Tom, I don't think you'll ever make Superintendent.'

Browne smiled sadly. 'Maybe you're right, sir.' If Petty were a typical one, he decided, maybe he wouldn't be sorry!

Chapter 13

In spite of Jennie's sanguine hopes, nothing Mitchell had heard from the walkers he had interviewed during the morning had been either interesting or exciting. He had enlivened his labours, though, with imaginary pictures of Rebel biting and snapping at court officials. He must look out for Col and hear what had happened. Now he wanted his lunch and he wanted it with Ginny. She wouldn't be expecting him so he'd better call at the Italian take-away.

When he presented the boxed pizzas, she was unenthusiastic. 'I'm trying to lose some weight.'

He laughed. 'Don't be ridiculous.'

'Well, you ought to be.'

Time to change the subject. 'Declan asleep?'

She nodded and looked alarmed as he went towards the child's bedroom door. 'For pity's sake don't wake him!'

Of course he wouldn't. He regarded his son with satisfaction. He had Ginny's hair, black and beginning to curl, and her pale complexion though he was flushed with sleep. He lay, arms outflung so that his upper and lower garments had parted company to reveal a baby's pot-belly.

Virginia had crept up behind him and now she stepped forward to point to it. 'They forget that when they say he's more like me than you.'

Mitchell was still in sentimental mood. 'Jennie's beginning to see what she's missing. She had it in mind for herself when she was here last week.'

'It's not in her mind, it's in her belly, due in December but that's a close secret as yet. Don't say anything at the station.'

Mitchell sighed. 'Ah well, it helps to make the world go round. She's a good copper. I hope she comes back afterwards. Come on. That food's getting cold.'

They ate at the kitchen table and discussed their respective mornings. Virginia had begun a Shakespeare essay.

'He wrote *A Midsummer Night's Dream*.'

'Thank you, Benny.' Solemnly.

'It's about...'

She noticed the derisive curl of his lip. 'I know what it's about, and before you start, I can imagine your opinion of it.'

'Well, give me yours. I'd be glad to hear from an intelligent person who has something to say in favour of it. Maybe it was his first effort.'

'It was his fifth.'

'Who'd have wanted to see it?'

'It was for the entertainment at an aristocrat's wedding. It's a good play for a school to put on, plenty of brilliant spectacle. The audiences of the time would have loved it. It's what they expected—in the tradition that Shakespeare inherited.'

'Inherited? Ah, you mean he got all his plots from somebody else?' He waved away her protests. 'Yes he did. He got *Macbeth* out of an old history book and I'm sure I've heard of this Theseus character somewhere else.'

Virginia smiled. Benny always covered his back in his forays into literary criticism

242

with an exaggerated display of ignorance. 'It must have something. It's the most frequently performed of the plays. It's been made into seven films and they're done it eight times on TV.' She stole an olive from the top of his pizza. 'There's even a jazz version with the Benny Goodman Sextet and Louis Armstrong as Bottom.'

Mitchell's interest was caught. 'I bet stuffed-shirt Hunter doesn't know that.'

'What's the school play like?'

'I'm no judge, but those who claim to be rate it.' He sat appreciating the casual grace of her movements as she set up the coffee machine.

She came back to the table and pushed the fruit bowl towards him. He took a banana without complaining. He supposed he could hardly expect to be offered chocolate cake after pizza. 'Tell me about the kids who are in it.'

Virginia had learned discretion as a policeman's daughter before she became a policeman's wife. He had no qualms about discussing the case with her fully, but as he began she shook her head. 'No, just tell me what they look like, what they're interested in, who's friendly with who. It might give me an idea to suggest and it might make you see them differently.'

Having devoured the banana, he cut an apple in four neat pieces and reconsidered. 'Michael Cunningham's the one who strikes you most forcibly. You can pick him out now as trouble. He has a whole different set of principles from a normal person. He stands back from the positive things normal people are trying to do and tweaks and twists them.' He demolished the first quarter of apple. 'The pity is that we'll have to wait till he's fulfilled our expectations and hurt someone seriously before we can bang him up.'

Virginia was startled. 'You seriously want the power to pluck out suspicious characters before they've offended?'

'I realize I can't have it but it makes you feel powerless, just waiting.'

'What's he done so far?'

'Very likely rigged the results of the school sports meeting we were reading about a fortnight ago.'

'Drugs?'

'He's got a Saturday job at Mason's.'

Virginia poured coffee. 'Do you really believe the world's divided into the criminal types and the others?'

Mitchell disposed of his coffee as he gave

his wife's question serious consideration. 'I don't think all crime is committed by people who are destined to do it. Circumstances have to make a difference. People are panicked into rash actions and sometimes giving way to selfish little impulses has more serious consequences than people expect. On the other hand I was pretty convinced by the stuff I read about the profiling of serial killers when we were on that choral society case two years ago. You can pick out people you can't reason with, who don't seem capable of being sorry or ashamed. They don't make the bulk of our customers by any means, but they're bound to end up either in serious trouble or so clever and successful that we know all about them but can't touch them. I think Michael's one of them.'

They drained the coffee pot as he offered thumbnail sketches of their various suspects, then cleared away the dishes as Virginia considered them. 'What about this Metcalfe? He was afraid Julia wanted to marry him and you've just accepted all he's told you. Maybe he followed her home when she changed her clothes—or met her again afterwards. One forty was a bit early to leave to be at Holmbrooke by two. What if he did it to get out of being sued for breach of promise? Or because she found out he was on all the drugs he pretended to be so shocked about? Maybe he's keeping them for Michael if they aren't in his house.' Her tone was not serious but her words supplied Mitchell with food for thought as he drove back to the station.

When the briefing began, he would have a suggestion ready to offer along with the purely negative results of listening to more than two hours of teenage chatter. That thought, together with the enjoyment of a meal with his family, had put Mitchell into an amiable frame of mind.

Unless there was an unexpectedly speedy conclusion to this case he would not be playing cricket on Saturday, but at least Virginia would video the county game for him to watch when he was free. He turned a corner and contemplated the large plot being weeded by a neighbour. As she rose to her feet with a pained expression and rubbed the small of her back, Mitchell even began to feel grateful for his flat where the garden, and therefore the gardening, was shared.

He quite liked digging and hoeing but

his duties as a DC, a husband, a father and one of the openers for the Cloughton force's First Eleven left too little time to be responsible for the half acre he planned to tackle when he retired.

When Browne invited him to address the team, he summarized the evidence of the nine walkers he had talked to in one sentence, then repeated Virginia's speculations. 'She wasn't entirely serious about Metcalfe as the killer, but we did just swallow the guff he gave us. Do we need to think again?'

Browne shook his head. 'If you felt you could believe him at the time, I should stick with your first impression. One of the differences between a good and a bad copper is knowing an honest witness when you talk to one—though no policeman's infallible, of course.'

Mitchell, anxious to clear up any doubts concerning Metcalfe, knew that Dean would be reluctant to demonstrate himself a 'bad copper' in the light of the definition just offered. He flashed an appeal to Browne who went on, 'On the other hand, a good copper is always double checking and is not unwilling where necessary to admit to a mistake. In any case, now we haven't found Michael's cache at home we can justify a search of the clubhouse. You can work on the rapport you've already got with Metcalfe to arrange that and reconsider the man himself as you go. You can have a couple of men to help you turn the place over.'

'What if Michael's anticipated all this searching?' Jennie asked, 'and is shifting the stuff around? It could even be back home again by now.'

Dean smiled. 'That would suit us very well. Denton would catch him in the act.'

Jennie persisted. 'If the Couriers' clubhouse proves a blank, what about the school? Michael probably has a locker there for his books and some space to keep things in the common room—or his desk even. He sounds brazen enough.'

Browne approved this suggestion. 'You've liaised with the school, Jerry. Can you persuade them nicely? Only get heavy if you have to.'

Apprised of Jennie's condition and concerned by the lethargy apparent in spite of her smiles and suggestions, he wondered how, tactfully, he could give her a task she felt up to.

248

'That leaves you at a loose end, Jennie. You've done your share of walkers for one day. Where do you feel you'd be most useful?'

Her grateful smile told him she was not deceived. 'I'd like another chat with Fiona Manley. I'll dream up an excuse on the way.'

Satisfied, Browne turned to Dean who reported on his harassment of Saxby with evident enjoyment. 'It would have been fun to find he was having it off with Julia, but I honestly didn't get that impression. He only got hysterical when I said we wanted to see Emma again.'

'Do we?'

'Not really, but I wanted to needle him. He said that she was in Manchester with Helen Rowe and a girl called Wendy and that Laura Saxby had taken them. I radioed Jerry to save him making a wasted journey, but apparently he'd already arrived and seen something interesting so he carried on.'

'Go on, Jerry.'

Hunter paused in his prowling round the office and perched on the window sill to give his report. 'There was movement in the house. I'd just got Richard's message when I caught a glimpse of Helen Rowe at the bedroom window.'

'Sure it was her?'

'Certain. She darted back when she saw me.'

'Did she know you'd seen her?'

'I'm not sure. I didn't mention it to Miss Saxby. I felt she was lying to me on occasions. She didn't seem happy with herself when she was talking about the girls' trip. She was much more relaxed when she was defending her brother against allegations of unfaithfulness. I agree with Richard that we're probably barking up the wrong tree there.'

'Why didn't you ask about Helen?'

'I thought I'd tackle the girl herself.'

'Not as quick with her inventions as Laura Saxby?'

'She's quick enough but I think Helen would be even more uncomfortable if she was telling less than the truth.'

Browne nodded. 'Well, you all seem to have a busy afternoon planned. Before you go, we have a few scraps from the forensic boys. The woollen cap, presumably Julia's, found beside the body had smears of make-up inside it that matched what was on her face. We saw that her jacket was wet and muddy. It also had pulled threads and little tears and rips in places, so we're looking for threads of red and blue polyester. Don't ask me where.'

'Tea party in Petty's room for you?'

'Afraid so, Jerry. And then I thought I might let Dr Travers hear the sound of his own voice.'

Browne had studied his reports until, if required, he felt he could recite them to Petty by heart. Since it was unlikely that the Superintendent would be impressed by this accomplishment, Browne reported his team's progress in the customary manner before setting out for Travers' surgery. He felt he had deserved this foray into the work he missed—on the hoof, out to the witnesses.

The tape was in his pocket and he knew that off by heart too. 'Don't contact me again...at least not on the same subject.' So, Travers had not been breaking off diplomatic relations, just making one topic taboo. 'The appointment's been made...' A medical one seemed most likely. Was it for Julia herself and she hadn't wanted to go? But she was being accused of interfering so it must have been for someone else.

Someone would be keeping an appointment that Julia wanted to prevent.

Whatever it was, Travers was in a position to take some official action to put an end to Julia's opposition. Browne had summoned Hilary Deakin to listen to the message but she had professed to be unable to help, beyond confirming that the voice was David Travers'. She had volunteered, though, that Julia had rung him and met him in the last week or two more frequently than she had before that. Was there anything there?

Travers certainly had not sounded over-friendly in his message. Had Julia been pursuing him? The impression of Julia that the investigation had given him so far made it seem unlikely. She was too conventionally—in these days, maybe unconventionally—moral and respectable. Had she weakened and had an affair with him that she now regretted? Was she trying to prevent him from meeting his lawyer to begin proceedings to dissolve his marriage?

He shook his head to clear it. He was getting silly, clutching at straws. It was not an affectionate message. Its tone was of patient exasperation—as though he felt that she might have a point even while his duty was to oppose her. He had listened so many times and the message was so short that he had read into it a myriad fanciful interpretations.

He had not yet met Travers. He speculated about what kind of man would have married a wife whose word in school was instantly obeyed, who could trek twenty miles through the night and still walk further only eight or nine hours later, who had Michael's seal of approval on her face and figure and Hunter's on her intelligent conversation. He proved to be tall, raw-boned and red-haired with an acne-scarred face. He moved athletically and his manner was direct but encouraging.

The practice waiting room was equipped with fresh flowers, magazines, pictures, toys and taped music, but the surgery into which Browne was shown was strictly functional. The surface of the desk from which the doctor turned was not visible. The overlapping papers in various pastel shades that covered it all had heavy print followed by a mixture of dotted lines and blank boxes. The medical profession obviously had its share of useless forms to fill in.

Travers' answers to Browne's preliminary questions were straightforward. Julia was not his patient. Kit was sorry about her death, particularly the manner of it, but was not unduly upset. Julia had been invited to the house when she first arrived in Cloughton—that was only polite—but she and Kit did not become close friends. He had made an effort to be friendly with Julia himself because she was Kit's relative. He had heard that she was more than competent in her work.

'You didn't find her a little overbearing? Interfering, perhaps?' Browne stressed his penultimate word.

Travers looked at him with distaste rather than consternation. 'Don't play games and waste my time. Just ask what you want to know.'

Chidden, Browne produced his tape. 'I haven't brought a machine. I don't suppose I need to play it to you.'

He shook his head briefly and still waited for Browne's direct question. When it came, he would only say that Julia had gained the confidence of one of his patients, taken it upon herself to disagree with his course of action on that patient's behalf, then presumed to harangue both

254

the patient and himself.

The two men glared at each other for some seconds before Browne asked, 'Is Fiona Manley one of your patients?'

He replied, stiffly, 'She's on the practice list.'

'I suppose it wouldn't be possible for you to tell me something about her condition and treatment?'

'You suppose right.' Browne thought that the doctor looked suddenly put out.

As the door closed behind the DCI some minutes later, Travers buzzed his receptionist. 'Bring me Fiona Manley's card in here, would you?'

Chapter 14

Dean set off for the sports shop Metcalfe ran in partnership with one of his fellow Couriers. He would soften up Metcalfe, he decided, by looking round his establishment for the new squash racquet he had been promising himself for some time.

He spent a few moments looking up

and down the unfrequented back-street in which he found the premises. The other buildings seemed to be offices and warehouses, though 'Sports Feet' did keep company with a run-down greengrocer's shop and a greasy-looking coffee bar. Still, business probably ticked over if the two men supplied all their fellow Couriers exclusively. A section of the small window display was given over to items in vivid gold with blue hoops, presumably the club strip. This had not been worn by the members he had mingled with on Monday but it would be required when representing the club.

When Dean entered and stated his business, Metcalfe's partner obligingly took charge of the shop. Since it was empty of customers, Dean found Metcalfe's thanks rather over-effusive. He went with him to the 'back room' which was a cross between a lobby and a cupboard, windowless with a partly dismantled gas fire that Dean thought would definitely be condemned by both the gas board and the fire service.

He explained, tactfully for him, that he was following up the activities of a Courier member. 'Not one of your golden boys, just a hanger-on, I think. You can expel him before it all blows up.'

Metcalfe seemed more intrigued than annoyed. 'We haven't many hangers-on.' He looked at Dean hopefully but received no response. Instead, the DC settled himself on the only chair and made an appeal of his own.

'Look, I could go in with a team of men and a big stick but neither of us has anything to gain from that approach. I thought you might guide me through the proper procedures to retain goodwill on both sides.' Dean smiled to himself. Browne would be proud of him.

Metcalfe was nodding importantly. 'It's the secretary who's the key man.' He sniffed. 'You know, he's not a yob like the rest of us—he can read and write and keeps reminding us about it. He doubles as our first aid officer.'

Dean's heart sank. Now he understood the reason for the edge to Metcalfe's voice. Doubtless he'd treble as the club's legal adviser on this occasion. 'Any chance of you coming along with me? You know, two yobs together against a representative of the educated classes. Safety in numbers.' Dean congratulated himself on his versatility. First the hit-man and now the diplomat!

It was clear that Metcalfe was his man. He supplied the secretary's number and offered the use of the shop's telephone. Now, Dean changed his ploy and with conspiratorial winks and sniggers at Metcalfe, he invited Charles Penrose, as his fellow upholder of the law, to help deal with this business, 'Keeping the lowest possible profile for the sake of the club's good name.'

It was arranged for the three men to meet at the club hut in thirty minutes' time. Dean passed fifteen of them spending rather more than he'd planned for an up-market racquet. This restored the smile to the face of the long-suffering partner left once more in charge of the shop.

Precisely on time, Penrose arrived with the club keys. On the journey, Metcalfe had refrained from pressing Dean for a name, probably anticipating a sharp answer. The solicitor had different expectations as he asked, conspiratorially, 'Which locker are we interested in?' The tone changed abruptly when Dean revealed that his men would want to see into all the lockers, cupboards and drawers, every nook and cranny—and, for good measure, to examine the walls and floorboards for signs of recent prising.

Dean himself began on the top row of lockers and the car containing his promised assistants arrived before he had completed the search of the second. He was not especially impatient to arrive at Michael's on the third row down. He considered the boy would be more likely to have planted the stuff in a generally used area than to have left it among his own possessions.

When the searchers did reach number twenty-two, Dean watched as they handled the malodorous socks, the girlie magazines and the items of female underwear quite impassively. It was Metcalfe who remarked, 'They obviously wouldn't pay their forfeits to get them back.'

The search was meticulous but no irregular substances were found and, after scrutinizing the floor, the men decided that the locker had not been tampered with. Dean made as much as he could of this. 'So glad not to have to cause any damage—though of course we always make good...able to keep it discreet...middle of the week with no spectators...very grateful for the time you've spared us.' There were smiles all round as the hut was locked up and everyone departed.

Dean was gloomy. Michael would have hidden the stuff at school and jammy Hunter would be the one to find it!

Jennie Taylor was fairly sure that the rapport she had established with Fiona Manley at her last visit would be such as to make her an acceptable visitor now. She rang the plastic bell-push on the plastic door just once, then stood in front of the window alongside it so that Fiona would see and recognize her.

A head appeared in the kitchen doorway, then disappeared again. A long pause followed. Jennie waited for Fiona to gather courage and refrained from ringing again. Then she stopped thinking about Fiona and clung to the door handle as a wave of dizziness and nausea swept over her.

After a minute the door was flung open and a totally new Fiona was drawing her in and placing her capably in an armchair. Jennie was glad that the ministrations stopped at that and she was given time and space to gather her wits. After several seconds, she looked up to find Fiona contemplating her so far unscratched wedding ring and her ashen face. 'You're pregnant, aren't you?'

The girl was a nurse. Jennie decided to turn a disadvantage into an asset, to let Fiona feel she was in charge and to indulge her symptoms rather than trying to conceal them. At the same time, through half-closed eyes, she took a quick look round. There were a crumpled paper and a chewed-looking ball-point pen on the table. Fiona had been labouring with them and drinking neat whisky, though apparently only in small quantities. The bottle was still almost full.

She answered with nods and murmurs Fiona's brisk questions. 'Happy about it? How far on are you? Any serious problems? Is it your first? And then, more sharply, 'When did you last eat?'

'Lunchtime, but it wasn't much more successful than at breakfast.'

Fiona nodded knowingly. 'You'll not want tea or coffee.'

Jennie answered with a slight shake of the head and an expression of horror. Fiona laughed and turned her back to reach into the kitchen cupboards. She placed on the table a packet of semi-sweet biscuits and a large bottle of fizzy lemonade.

'I don't think...'

'Try it!'

Through her own temporary distress, Jennie was aware of Fiona's more serious troubles—a capable, assertive woman, rendered useless by this mysterious, intangible complaint. Fiona poured the liquid and she drank some of it, finding to her astonishment that her stomach accepted it. Suddenly, she felt on top of the world. 'I feel...'

'Yes, I know. I've seen it all before.'

'Tell me about it.'

Totally relaxed, Fiona did, describing her training, a spell as a district midwife and the position as part of the theatre staff in the gynaecological unit at Cloughton Royal Hospital that she'd had to give up. She finished sadly. 'If Adrian hadn't assured me he'd take on all financial responsibility till I'd recovered, I think I might have stuck it out.

'We'd both have been better off. I'd have had a distraction from my wretched fears—or else I'd have been forced to admit to them and get some sort of treatment. He could have indulged his fantasies about Julia without agonizing over being disloyal to me. I've treated him pretty shabbily. Now I've decided that it's got to stop.'

She picked up the lemonade and offered to refill the glass but Jennie shook her head. 'I saw the specialist my doctor referred me to yesterday,' Fiona continued. 'It was a lot easier talking to him than I'd expected. He thought I might have a problem with gross muscle co-ordination, eye muscle movement in particular. It means that to focus my eyes on an object costs me a great deal of unconscious effort.

'The specialist came to see me at home. I deliberately fixed it for a schoolday and didn't tell Adrian. I couldn't bear the thought of being cross-examined about it. The doctor said the brain can compensate to some extent but sometimes it can only cope by producing symptoms like mine. In the end I managed to get down to his clinic in his car.

'It was such a relief to find that, probably, it all has a physical cause. I'm not just neurotic and I'm not going mad and I don't have to force myself to cross roads or do charity walks. I only have to do daily breathing and eye exercises and wear a patch over one eye when no one else is around. I think I'm even ready to face a few jokes about parrots and pirates.'

'What does Adrian think?'

She looked guilty but determined. 'I haven't told him about any of it. For two days I've been trying to screw myself up to telling him I'm leaving.' She leaned forward and adopted her staff nurse attitude again. 'If you're feeling better, perhaps you'd better ask me what you came to ask and then we can both get on with our own affairs.'

'Just one more question before we change the subject. Did Julia offer any opinion about all these new plans and treatments?'

Fiona's face darkened. 'I didn't tell her anything about it either. Julia's "help" sabotaged every effort I made to get myself together over the last few months. It's having her off my back that's lifted the pressure enough for me to come so far.'

Hunter ran Mr Gregson to earth in the staff room and was immediately taken to task for attending the play rehearsal on Wednesday without his permission. 'I'd have expressed my unwillingness to have you there at the time if you'd had the courtesy to let me know you were in school.'

Hunter was meticulously polite. 'We tried to do that, sir. DC Mitchell came to the staff room and I tried your office. When we both drew a blank, we thought it most likely that you were in the school hall, encouraging such staff as were valiantly keeping afloat a school play deprived of its producer. However, Mr Naylor told me that you had gone home.'

There were subdued sniggers from such staff as were free to listen. Considering honours were about equal, Hunter returned to the brief Browne had given him. He had not made a very auspicious start and he anticipated a furious outburst from Gregson, followed by a refusal when he made his request to search through Michael Cunningham's possessions.

The headmaster retreated instead into a cold reasonableness. 'If the finger of suspicion points to us then I shall offer every co-operation to prove our innocence. I insist that you search not only this pupil's private...er, the areas allocated to Michael to store his possessions—but that you treat us all alike.'

Maybe provoked by some of his staff's horrified faces, he added, 'The staff too.' These were the teachers who had laughed at him only a minute ago. 'I assure you, Sergeant Hunter, none of us has anything to hide.' Hunter read in all the faces of all the staff present the opinion that this was a rash and foolish declaration.

He resisted the temptation to tell Mr Gregson that his work would go ahead irrespective of any insistence or objection. The head, for his own reasons, had given willing permission for more than the police, at present, had the right to ask. He would avail himself of the offer and see what it turned up.

At three o'clock, Fiona Manley closed the door on DC Taylor's cheerful farewell. 'I don't know what Paul's going to think of fizzy pop for breakfast. Anyway, I wish you all the best for your new plans.'

For a minute or so she walked up and down the hall, listening to Jennie's retreating footsteps and talking silently to herself. It was go now or stay for ever. She mustn't be here when Adrian came home after his meeting. She'd never be able to find the words to speak to him. She hoped he would understand why her message had to be in writing. She returned to the kitchen table and spent

266

a further half hour composing it, lowering the level of the whisky about an inch in the process. It made her more fluent if not more lucid.

She tried to imagine Adrian's reaction when he saw the note and read it through. 'I've probably done you irreparable harm. I've certainly used you, presumed on your good nature, accepted your generosity, knowing that I didn't feel anything stronger than friendship for you. I've deprived you of Julia who might have felt more.

'Now I'm creeping off, taking the coward's way out, unable to face you. I only know I must go. For my own sake, I have to prove I can survive without a stranglehold on someone else. For your sake, I have to leave room for a real relationship and put an end to the lie we're living.'

She wrinkled her nose. The last sentence in particular offended her. It was melodramatic, to put it mildly, but it was the best way she could express it and there was no more time left to start again. Now she must pack.

Clothes were no problem; they would be no use to him. The bedding was his and he could keep the odd towel that was hers.

She might as well take back all the small ornaments he had ferried over for her. He was hardly going to want them to remind him of her.

What about the things he had bought her whilst she was contributing nothing to the budget. To leave them was ungracious and to take them was greedy and unjustified. She had better leave those things he might be able to use. She would take no books except her nursing text books and the paperback science-fiction that he disliked.

She wrapped carefully the picture that had been her last present from her grandfather before he died but left the two watercolours Adrian had bought for her when she moved in, her 'welcoming present'. She had no compunction about taking back all her compact discs. Adrian was practically tone deaf. It was one reason why she had never felt comfortable in his house. Her music was a great help and consolation and she felt guilty if she played it when he was in, knowing that he would prefer a talk on the radio or a film on television.

It amused Fiona to use the suitcase on wheels for its proper purpose. None of the neighbours would gossip about her moving out because she hardly ever left the house without it. She wished she could think of somewhere to go other than her own flat. It was the first place he would look for her. She had no illusions that he would submit to the request in her letter to be left alone to learn to stand on her own feet.

She rang for a taxi, then stood looking out of the front window, reflecting on all the times she had dreaded walking outside into the world it revealed. She was not sure if she could do it now, but she did know that she had a physical problem, the strain from which had probably caused her psychological one. If her horrors came on her when she went out there she would just begin her breathing exercises. If the passers-by thought she was mad, it didn't matter now that she knew she wasn't.

The taxi drew up. She was aware of her erratic pulse as she set off, but she made it down the path and across the pavement to where the driver held the door open for her.

Julia was dead and she had left Adrian. Now she would never have to answer to 'Fi' again.

Chapter 15

Browne walked back to his office oblivious of the June sunshine, meditating on Travers' refusal to divulge Fiona Manley's medical problems. He became aware of it only as it dazzled him at his desk facing the window. For the first time since an overalled workman had appeared to fix it he saw some point in the new venetian blind and adjusted the slats to take away some of the glare before placing his jottings on Travers with the other notes in the case file. He expected to be undisturbed for the next hour or so. His team had been instructed to report all the afternoon's negative findings by telephone from home. A personal appearance would herald an exciting development. Seeing no notes on his desk he rang down to reception to ask for his messages. Bennett sounded surprised to hear his voice.

'Didn't know you were back, sir. Did you use the back stairs? There's a Mr Naylor waiting to see you. Wants to confess to killing Julia Feather.'

'Naylor?'

'That's what he said. Spotty, dark-haired chap carrying a briefcase.'

'What have you done with him so far?'

'Nothing except leave him to cool his heels in number four.'

'Send in some tea and just leave him there—for another hour at least. If he changes his mind before that and wants to leave, let him go and follow him.' Browne sighed and rang for coffee, answered a call from the frustrated Dean, then settled down to peruse the report on Fiona Manley.

He thought it unlikely that Naylor really had murder on his conscience. The question was, did he just think Fiona was guilty or had he reason to know she was? Julia had supplied her with unwanted, insensitive help. She represented a threat too of replacing Fiona in Adrian's affections which would deprive her of a protector more to her liking. His speculations on her opportunity to commit the murder were interrupted by the arrival of Hunter, looking well pleased with life.

Browne waved him to an armchair, acquainted him with the latest development and shared with him his own speculations. 'Not a shred of evidence we have so far points to Naylor. With luck, when he's waited long enough he'll have second thoughts and go home.'

Hunter nodded thoughtfully, then reached into his briefcase. He produced a plastic evidence bag containing a large zip-up pencil case and dangled it in front of Browne's face.

Browne regarded it solemnly. 'Open it then.'

Hunter shook out the case and unzipped it using the only tools he had in his pocket, a penknife and a roller-ball pen. Inside, in two clear plastic packages, Browne saw yellow layered tablets and capsules, one end clear, the other opaque blue.

'So they were in Michael's school locker.'

'No.' Hunter anchored the case with his penknife and re-zipped it with the end of his pen. 'Naylor's.'

Since Naylor had displayed a taste for melodrama, the two officers had decided to indulge him and Browne walked in on him swinging the plastic bag from its string. The sight that met him almost persuaded him to abandon the plan. Number four was their most depressing interview room, its walls a dirty buff, its concrete floor dark blue in the few places where the paint had not worn away. It contained only a table, rickety and marked with white rings from hot cups, and two chairs. The ash tray was empty but the air smelt of stale cigarette smoke. Naylor sat patiently on one of the chairs, his head bowed and his hands folded, like a monk at his office. He looked up and, seeing what Browne carried, he started up. 'Don't forget I came to tell you about it before I knew you'd found anything.'

Hunter smiled. 'You were in the staff room. Are you telling me you didn't hear the Head's invitation to search the whole school?'

Naylor declined to answer and buried his head in his hands. The two policemen watched him and waited. Eventually, without raising his head, he began his self-justification. 'It seemed a heaven-sent chance. I've had discipline problems ever since I started work. I hadn't the right personality to be a good teacher. I'm not dominating. I don't expect a class to do what I say and it doesn't. And then this lecturer came along and actually named substances that could change your very nature, make you feel confident and full of assurance. It would be a sort of treatment to help me be like the rest of the staff.'

'Is that what Michael called it?'

'No, he waited about till his friends had gone, then he hung round my car till I came out. He said, "Fancy a bit of a trip, sir? You only live once you know." That's what got to me. This was the only existence I was going to have and it was hell. The juniors rioted round me, though the sixth-form didn't. In this school you win popularity by hard work and success, but they had long memories and they made it plain with various snide comments that they were working and behaving themselves because they wanted to and not because I'd learned how to make them.'

Hunter asked. 'Wouldn't it have been better to get to know yourself, value yourself as you are and change to a more suitable occupation?'

'Like writing? I've been wanting to do that. I've got plenty of interesting things to write about. I can see further into things than the loud-mouths who are held in high esteem at Holmbrooke because they can shout and scare the children into good behaviour.' His scorn for his colleagues' intellectual paucity matched his bitterness at his pupils' disregard. 'They haven't anything worthwhile or interesting to say when they've got them sitting quietly. They just make heavy use of text books and pass on borrowed ideas. At least I have my own even if I haven't got what it takes to claim people's attention and make them listen to me.'

'And did it work?' Naylor looked at Browne, puzzled. 'The pills. Did they give you this magic ability to dominate children?'

His voice rose hysterically. 'No, they made me kill Julia!'

'Really? Do you remember doing it?'

Browne watched Naylor as he hesitated, perhaps wondering if a vaguely negative answer might lead to a plea of diminished responsibility. Eventually he said, 'Not the details.'

Hunter's voice came from behind Browne. 'Do you remember mopping up the blood and getting rid of the stained clothes you were wearing?'

'Yes, but only vaguely. I'd been drinking as well.'

'I see. What about a weapon?'

'I used a knife.'

'Naturally. Describe it.'

'Well, it was an ordinary knife. A sharp one.'

Browne gave a bark of grim laughter. 'Where did all this take place? At your house?' He nodded. 'And where was Miss Manley?'

'Well, she was out.'

'Out?' They all sat silent, contemplating this absurdity. Then Naylor rallied. 'Why not? She's out now. She's just left me a note and walked out on me...' He stopped speaking, realizing he might be destroying Fiona's defence. Hurriedly he returned to a former topic. 'How could I be a writer? I'd hardly earn enough to feed and clothe myself. There's nothing but teaching that I would be qualified to do that would keep Fiona as well at a reasonable standard. I have to think of her.'

'No you don't. She has no claim on you. You might even be preventing her recovery. If she needed to keep herself she might become involved in her work again and distracted from her symptoms.'

'You don't understand...'

Browne thought he did. For this inadequate man who could find little intrinsic value within himself, Fiona represented a worthwhile cause that justified his existence. She had left him, demonstrating her ability to manage alone, but he would go after her because of his need of her. Naylor was still speaking. 'What happens to me now—as far as the police are concerned?'

Browne swallowed his exasperation. 'If we graciously waive the charge of wasting police time with false confessions it leaves you certainly accused of possession—a peccadillo, I suppose, in a murder investigation, but your headmaster won't look too kindly on it. Why on earth were you storing the stuff? That might leave you open to charges of pushing. You were definitely aiding and abetting Michael.'

The hysteria was back. 'He came round to the house in the evening on the day you turned the Cunningham place over. He said you'd get round to all his other hidey-holes at your own moderate pace so I'd have to keep it for him. He said not to try any tricks because he'd counted everything carefully. I couldn't keep it at the house. Fiona might have found it—or you might and that could have made you suspect her.'

Browne sighed. 'Go home, Naylor, and write a novel.'

Naylor went out, walking with a dejected droop. After escorting him through the foyer, Hunter returned to Browne's office. 'Jennie saw Fiona Manley this afternoon. Shall I see if she knows where she's gone?'

'Yes, but first can you get round to Naylor's place and get that note Fiona left before he has a chance to destroy it. If she can take off and leave him today she could well have taken off and knifed Julia on Sunday. She might even have made a confession herself.'

'You don't think she is agoraphobic?'

'Oh, I'm sure she is but a major panic can override a minor one. I've got one or two things to see to, and then I think we need a drink. Meet you in the Fleece in an hour?'

Hunter nodded. 'Let's ask Benny.' Browne looked doubtful and Hunter realized he could offer his son-in-law no privileges.

'All right, but we'll ask Jennie and

Richard as well. I'll phone them. Better bring your notebook. We might find Saxby there, waiting to treat us to his confession.'

At nine o'clock Mitchell and Hunter joined Browne in his favourite bar in the Fleece. The sergeant answered Browne's raised eyebrows. 'Jennie's gone to bed—she's not well—and Richard's at his mother's birthday party.' This reason for absence from the unfilial Dean caused amusement to all three of them. 'Jennie admits she can't stand the pace,' Mitchell announced, wriggling his substantial form on to the upholstered seat behind the bay table. 'Richard has to find a fancy excuse.'

Hunter disappeared in the direction of the bar.

'Friday tomorrow,' remarked Browne. 'There's always an exception to prove the rule, but I think we'll either crack this case over the weekend or else it's going to drag on for months.'

As usual the six-foot-four-inch Hunter had signalled his request over the other customers' heads and been served quickly. He placed pints of best in front of his companions and sipped his half of draught cider. Mitchell regarded it suspiciously.

'The horse that passed that wasn't fit for work,' he pronounced and drank deeply at his own glass. Hunter merely grinned and began, for Mitchell's benefit, an account of Fiona Manley's flit and Naylor's confession. 'Morally,' he remarked in conclusion, 'Naylor may have done as much to harm Michael as Fiona.'

Mitchell shook his head. 'No one leads Michael astray. He's just a bad apple. Going along with him or not isn't going to make any difference.'

Browne stopped this argument impatiently. 'We haven't time to discuss criminal psychology. We've got a case to solve. What do we know about these drugs? Would they have given Naylor the nerve to knife someone who'd found him out?'

'You're asking me?'

Browne grinned at his sergeant. 'I'm just thinking aloud. Julia was at the lecture—she set it up. She'd have noticed that he asked all those questions.'

'And'—Mitchell took his nose out of his glass to make his contribution—'Naylor was very late picking Fiona up from church. Did he really take a crowd of children home? We ought to check.'

'Your first job tomorrow.'

Mitchell made a note of it, then scratched his head. 'Even if you're daft enough to think you'll be believed,' he asked no one in particular, 'why confess to protect a woman who's upped and left you?'

Browne explained at length his assessment of the relationship. 'If he doesn't believe she'll be lost without him and find she needs to come back, he'll have nothing else left.'

'If he needs a lame duck, what's the attraction of Julia?'

'Ah,' Browne smiled. 'She was the right woman for the man he wishes he was.'

'It's all right to discuss general psychology then?'

Browne was quick with his apology for this anomaly.

Hunter was looking puzzled. 'I've been looking through your notes on Travers. What could Julia possibly have gained from interfering with Fiona's medical treatment? I know she seems to have been bossy and domineering but she surely didn't feel qualified to overrule a GP's recommendation. And what was wrong with the treatment the consultant advised? From what Fiona said to Jennie, it seems pretty unexceptionable. Why shouldn't Fiona do exercises? It wasn't as though she'd been put on controversial drugs with unknown side-effects. You don't think anyone had got Fiona to try the stolen stuff and Julia knew about that?'

'No chance. She was a nurse.'

Browne nodded and despatched Mitchell to collect the next round. 'We'd be nearer to who,' he observed to Hunter, 'if we could work out where. There was hardly any bleeding and what little blood there was soaked into her thick jacket so there are no pools or stains to alert us. There's some evidence that she was sitting in a chair at the point when rigor reached her arms but she was moved before it got to her legs. That doesn't help much. And a knife's not an easy weapon to look for. A quick wash and it can go back where it belongs. The one we're interested in has probably had umpteen washes.' They sat silently puzzling until Mitchell came back with his round. Seven inches shorter than Hunter, he had his own methods for obtaining rapid service.

'We've never thought about our customer being someone totally unconnected with Cloughton.'

'My, Benny, you've been thinking and queueing at the same time! And you're right—at least, we've certainly never talked about it.'

Mitchell handed over Hunter's second cider with no slighting reference to it. 'Julia's travelled around a bit. Maybe we could visit some of the places she's taught and lived in in the last three years.'

'Wonderful. Petty's going to like that idea when you suggest it in the morning. "We're all off to different counties, sir, to dig up Julia's past." '

Mitchell was not pleased. 'You're handing over tomorrow's briefing to the Super?'

'I'm off to the college in Wakefield. Interviewing. We'll have to see if we can't get some young hopefuls into the force who can show you lot a thing or two. Actually,' he added hastily as both his subordinates made threatening gestures, 'you're doing pretty well. On our last murder investigation we had Nigel and Robin on the team. This time we're two experienced detectives short with not even a raw recruit to replace either of them.' He looked round ostentatiously then winked at Hunter.

'Who are you looking for?'

'Saxby. He's late coming in with his confession. Just a minute, though. We've got Kit Travers and the good doctor instead.' The other two turned to watch the pair settle themselves on the other side of the room. 'They don't seem to be on the best of terms either.'

Mitchell brightened. 'Do we creep up and listen?'

'We sit as far out of sight as possible and keep our beady eyes open. If they spot us we wave and offer them a drink. We'll keep their goodwill—at least as much of it as is left. We might need it later. What is it, Jerry?'

Hunter assumed a deferential expression. 'I believe it's your round, sir.'

Browne obliged. When he came back he found Mitchell had appointed himself leader of the triumvirate. 'What have we got on all these people? Who are you backing, Jerry?'

Hunter hid his amusement behind his refilled glass before replying with deadly seriousness. 'I'm split between Michael himself and Daniel Stevens. I think it would be fairly easy to decide one way or the other about Daniel. In view of his home situation we've all gone rather easy on him but he's got to have the hard word soon and I think if he's done it he'll easily break. I'm pretty certain he's a customer of Michael's and I think a good deal of his motive would be at all costs to prevent his mother from being hurt when she finds he's cheated to win his races. Am I allowed to back Michael as well?'

'This isn't a party game,' Browne put in irritably. 'Oh well, go on.'

'Well, we've enough now to nail him for dealing. Naylor will give evidence when we've threatened him. Daniel might and there's Richard's evidence on the break-in. I think Michael is quite capable of killing but I'm not sure he did it. I think he'd be contemptuous of Julia's threat to expose him rather than afraid. That's if she did threaten him.'

'What about opportunity?'

'He seems to run fairly wild. His parents won't be able to tell us where he was and when and it won't be much use asking Paul.'

Mitchell drained his glass. 'Didn't someone suggest the other day that we should consider the parents of these children? Julia was very likely on to one or more of them. What would they do if it were

Tim or Fliss who was involved?' Hunter scowled. 'I don't mean I think they would be,' Mitchell went on hastily. 'Alex and Virginia—and Declan come to that—are all the wrong age to be found out by a teacher—but suppose your two had done something. Wouldn't you want to deal with it yourself, keep the school out of it, keep the police out of it? You'd make sure you put a stop to it but you'd be very anxious to keep it quiet.'

'I suppose I would.'

'Well, Julia doesn't seem to have been very good at keeping quiet.'

'Who's your favourite then, Benny? Still Hilary Deakin?'

Mitchell shrugged. 'Why did she say her boyfriend delivered her to school?'

'Because that's what she'd said to Kit Travers and she didn't want to admit to the row they'd had. It was silly though. She must see it's important. But why should she want to harm Julia? She could kick her out any time she wanted without killing her.'

'Unless it was about her that Hilary and lover boy quarrelled. If you don't want me to back her, I'll choose Saxby.'

'Why?'

Mitchell laughed. 'Because he's an irritating beggar. Because he had his photograph taken with Julia. Because it's damned uncivil of him to have been abroad when we want him here to be blamed.'

'There is that business between Laura Saxby and Helen Rowe to be explained.'

'Agreed,' Browne granted, 'but it's very likely nothing at all to do with him.'

'That leaves our friends over there.' Hunter nodded across the room in the direction of the corresponding bay to their own.

Mitchell poked his head out to look. 'They're having quite a set-to, but quietly.'

'We won't break Travers down.' Of that Browne was sure. 'Hilary probably warned them that we have the tape. I wonder if his wife knows about it?'

'Maybe that's what they're fighting about.' This idea seemed to please Mitchell. 'Maybe she thinks her bloke and Julia were having an affair.'

Browne sighed. 'Maybe she did, Benny. Perhaps you'd better add her to your list.'

'Who's your culprit, sir?'

'I always go for the unstable ones so I'm looking hard at both Naylor and Fiona.

Did Jennie know where Fiona had gone?'

Hunter shook his head. 'Couldn't ask her. Jennie had gone to bed and Paul refused to wake her up. Don't say I should have pushed him. He's as tall as me and as broad as Benny! Is Hannah still kindly driving us home?' Browne nodded. 'Well, it's my shout again. Let's see if switching to shorts throws a new light on things.'

Chapter 16

The Friday morning briefing was not a happy occasion for any of the people involved in it. Even Mitchell's head was sore, though he found some comfort in the knowledge that the responsibility for their indisposition lay chiefly with live-by-the-rule-book Hunter.

Jennie had failed to appear. 'It had better be something serious,' Petty had growled, but even he had sensed the waves of resentment the remark had caused and done his best to retrieve the situation. 'Only joking, of course. It's just that she's the sort of officer we can't afford to be without.'

Mitchell smiled to himself. It was certainly something with far-reaching consequences. He found he was very concerned for Jennie. After all, she'd been turned on to the idea by the charms of his own offspring. Well, perhaps that thought was just a mite conceited. He allowed that Jennie might have been following a fairly universal plan. He still hoped, though, that apart from immediate discomfort, all was well with her. Nothing trivial would have kept her away from work at any time.

He re-focused his attention on Petty, who was making jocular remarks about seeing people in the round. He must know that Jennie was pregnant. He was busy searching the sheets in Browne's case file.

'There isn't much in the CI's notes about Miss Feather's car. Red Fiat, wasn't it? Who's following it up?'

Hunter sounded apologetic. 'Well, we're all keeping our eyes and ears open but no one in particular is.'

Petty mimed astonishment and grief. 'No one is following up the car?'

'We all are, sir.'

'You all are today, that's for sure.' He glared at them in turn. 'You'll knock on all the doors along the route from Miss Deakin's house to this child's home—the one she was supposed to collect. You'll visit all the local garages, all the town car parks to talk to their attendants. You'll liaise with the traffic police...' He scribbled angrily on their action sheets, leaving indentations on the surface of the desk through three thicknesses of paper.

Mitchell was the one to interrupt him. 'Last night the CI told me to start with checking that Naylor actually delivered those children—'

The pen froze as Petty directed the full force of his displeasure on Mitchell. 'Yesterday afternoon the CI asked me to conduct his briefing. Inconvenient though I find it, I intend to accede to his request.' Mitchell met the glare without flinching and accepted the sheet that despatched him on a tour of the town's garages. The rest of them took their own without comment.

'I can't believe'—the Superintendent's tone was deeply ironic—'that the absence of any report on the weapon means that "no one in particular" has been looking for that.'

The remnants of the team looked

290

hopefully at the intrepid Mitchell. 'Where do you suggest we start, sir?' he asked innocently.

They watched in silence as Petty worked out that the SOC had not been pinpointed and that knives are easily washed and replaced. He resorted once more to his own brand of irony. 'That's your problem. Mine seems to be how to improve the basic selection and training of CID recruits.' Seeming pleased with this exit line, he departed with sad shakings of the head.

Hunter accepted his lot philosophically. Chatting to the regulars at the Red Lion would make a change from searching schools and listening to bogus confessions. He doubted that anything they told him would move the case any further along but his subconscious could be sifting more useful evidence. It was a pleasant morning. He would walk and let the fresh air cure his headache.

The landlord showed no resentment at a further catechism, even though Hunter declined a half pint on the house to assist him in putting his questions. 'A bit of gossip to chew over makes folk thirsty.' He took the DS to the exact spot where the Fiat had been found. 'It has to have been driven in from the Red Lion Lane entrance to be facing that way. I suppose it's possible to have come in from the other side but it would be very awkward. I've told a constable all this already.'

Hunter gritted his teeth. 'Yes, I know. Just double-checking.'

'That means it must have come from the posh end of town. If someone had driven it from one of the estates behind the station—from the grotty end—they'd have had to go round three sides of the one-way system, miles out of the way. I suppose you want to check again on the folk who were in on Sunday night and Monday dinner.'

'Please, and Sunday lunchtime as well if you can remember.'

He looked doubtful. 'It was a Bank Holiday.'

Frantic searching of the memory seldom produced the required information. Hunter spoke easily. 'Let's work backwards. Can you tell me exactly when you realized the car had been left? Did you ring us immediately?'

He shook his head. 'There was a spell of half an hour or so with no customers towards the end of Monday afternoon.' He glanced out of the window at the end of the bar and looked down on the now-empty car park, obviously repeating his action at the time he referred to. 'I remember it was there then but I assumed that it had been left by somebody who'd gone over the limit and would be coming back for it. I didn't think much about it till I noticed it was still there on Tuesday.

'I've given your other constable some names. I don't know which people he talked to but I've still got the rough list I made.' He rummaged in a drawer and produced a crumpled paper. 'Bill Chapman was last out on Sunday night. That I do remember.'

Hunter remembered too. Notes in the file told him that Chapman and his business partner had spent a long evening working out their financial problems in convivial surroundings and out of the earshot of their wives. Chapman was certain that the car park was quite empty once his own car had been driven away. He had insisted that he was sober and clear-headed. 'My work depends on my licence. I'd hardly risk it for the sake of an extra pint.'

He'd been back again for Monday

lunch—very early because it was a holiday and he had not booked a table—and this time with his wife in tow. Only four or five other cars were there, one of them a red Fiat parked at 'the Green Royd end'.

'Tell you what,' the landlord observed, looking pleased with himself. 'First customer on Monday morning was another customer from that school—Phil Brooke, he's the music master.'

This had not been in the notes. Hunter asked, 'Why on earth didn't you say so before?' and received the classic answer.

Mitchell was no more hopeful of spending a useful morning than his DS. He bargained with himself. Token visits to four garages should be rewarded by coffee and whatever else was on offer at his sleazy 'caff'.

At the first three, he was informed with varying degrees of politeness that there were a lot of Fiat Unos on the road, a lot of them were red and, unless they were brought in for some reason, no note was made of their registrations. The fourth one, 'Jack Schofield and Nephew', some considerable distance from either Hilary Deakin's house or Holmbrooke school, proved to Mitchell's great surprise to be the one chosen by Julia to service her vehicle regularly.

The nephew and namesake introduced himself and showed Mitchell into a small office containing a desk and two chairs on castors. The desk was covered in job-sheet books and order pads and a carousel card index of customers. There seemed not to be very many of them. Mitchell walked over dirty brown carpet tiles to the chair Schofield indicated and looked around. The walls were breeze block and gaps in the top coat of emulsion paint revealed countless coats beneath, with the smoke staining worse above each chair.

He phrased his question carefully, having no wish to sink deeper into Petty's displeasure by being reported for insolence to a witness. 'I'm sure the service you offer is excellent but why did Miss Feather come to you? It's not very handy, is it?'

The man was not in the least put out. 'No, I wondered myself at first, but it's Chris.'

'Chris?'

'He goes to her church. A few months ago the firm was going through a very sticky patch and I had to tell him I couldn't keep him. He talked to Jules about it and next thing I knew she was on the phone. Said she sympathized with my difficulties but if I could see my way to keep Chris on, I could count on her custom and she'd do her best to persuade her friends to come to me too.'

'And you took her seriously?'

He shrugged and grinned deprecatingly. 'I wanted to. I didn't really want to lose the lad. He's a good worker and if times got better I'd have been sorry I didn't struggle on with him. Jules' offer swung it.'

'And was she as good as her word?'

'Sort of. She brought several people but they didn't stay with us long. Not that there was anything wrong with our work, mind, but they were all people she lived near or worked with and we weren't conveniently placed for them. We're getting by now, though.'

'Can I see Chris?'

Schofield led the way into the workshop. Mitchell, looking round, thought Schofield had been over-sanguine. There were only a couple of vehicles on which work was currently being done, the ramp was empty and the three vans with the garage logo on the doors looked rusty and run down. Two youths stood about, one aimlessly whistling. The other, pad in hand, was checking spares. 'Which is he?'

Schofield grimaced. 'The one who's found himself something to do but the rule is last in first out.' He addressed the preferred youth. 'Fuzz to see you about Jules' car, Chris. You can use the office if it doesn't take too long.'

To Mitchell's surprise, the boy did remember seeing the Fiat on Sunday lunchtime, turning out at the end of Julia's road in the direction of Holmbrooke. 'You live round there?'

Chris blushed. 'No. As a matter of fact, I rather fancied her. She only sees me either here, in filthy overalls, or at church. I was dressed up and hanging about trying to decide whether to call and ask her out.'

'You're sure it was her car and she was driving?'

'Certain about both. We'd had the car in for servicing on Friday and she had complained that it sometimes wouldn't start. I renewed the spark plug leads and did an oil change, I couldn't find anything else wrong with it. It's newish—though she'd given it some hammer—and it didn't need anything. I was glad to see it had started that morning at least.'

'You can't remember the mileage on it, can you?'

'As a matter of fact, I can remember it exactly.' He was pleased with himself. 'It would have been hard to forget. Eleven thousand one hundred and eleven, all ones.' Mitchell consulted his notes. Now the milometer read one thousand one hundred and fourteen. It was two miles from the garage to Hilary's house and just over one mile from there to school. The car must have been parked somewhere along the route.

After a minute or two, Mitchell dismissed the lad and paused at the desk to record what he had learned. Glancing at the opposite wall, he admired a generously endowed, topless female wielding a huge spanner. Alone in the office with her, he blew her a kiss before making for the door.

Back at headquarters, Mitchell hoped his CI would have returned to receive his report but was resigned to handing it to Petty if he had to. He was even determined to hold his tongue in the face of the Superintendent's disparaging remarks. After all, he had a wife and a son to keep and it was becoming time to think seriously about his promotion.

His good intentions and stirring ambitions, however, were not destined to be noted by either of these superior officers. The only man on the case that he could find in the building was Dean, who was waiting, not very patiently, to report on his questioning of Julia's immediate neighbours.

Mitchell took his colleague's questions to be rhetorical. 'What are we supposed to do now? Hang around here till he deigns to dismiss us? If we go home we'll be for the high jump and if we wait around here we'll be in bother for wasting time!'

Mitchell was unsympathetic. 'You'll have to think of something. While you were partying last night, the CI told me to check that Naylor actually did deliver children home after Sunday's rehearsal. I don't see how I can go wrong doing that next.'

'You'd better have this then.' Dean fished a slip of paper out of his notebook. 'A Mrs Purley at number fifteen, opposite Hilary Deakin's, says that somebody from Julia's school called at the house at about a quarter to two. "Not too tall, dark hair, navy jacket." She's seen him before. Drove a white Fiesta. Doesn't Naylor? When he got no answer he jumped back into the car and drove off "at a rather silly speed".'

Mitchell accepted the scribbled note. 'Thanks.' The two constables called at Browne's office where they had standing permission to go in to look for messages. The top of the desk was empty. Mitchell grinned. 'That's for the Super's benefit. I bet it'll take him a while to sort out what he's swept into his drawers.'

Mitchell wandered downstairs, planning his first move. A telephone call to Kit Travers seemed a good idea. She would have known her cousin well enough to realize that some youngsters might be dependent on her for a lift home. She was not likely to have left without checking for small strays abandoned in the car park.

Kit Travers assured him that certainly she had not. She had spoken to the whole cast and been assured that no one was stuck for a lift. 'Amanda Richards half raised her hand and then changed her mind but in the end she travelled with us anyway. There wasn't anyone who didn't get home safely. I've seen them all since.'

Mitchell assured her that her provision had been quite adequate. 'Did Mr Naylor give anyone a lift?'

She was adamant. 'Definitely not. I marched them all out of school and the whole lot of them had dispersed before he came out. I specially looked because he just refuses to acknowledge the unwisdom of having a child alone in the car with him. Is there a problem, Constable Mitchell?'

He told her he was merely engaged in tedious routine checking, keeping his quickening interest out of his voice. So, Naylor had lied. Where had he been? If Browne was right about his relationship with Fiona Manley and her importance to Naylor's self-respect, what was important enough to keep the man from arriving on time at Dicky Birds? He wasn't going to waste time asking him. There wasn't much hope of a truthful answer after the rigmarole he'd entertained them all with last night. He'd work round to it obliquely, see what he could trick out of him.

He settled himself into his car and glanced at his watch. Three fifty. Lessons would be over at four o'clock, later than at most Cloughton schools. If he stepped on it he'd catch Naylor before he left. It was pretty canny of him to confess to killing Julia in a manner and place so unlikely. They'd maybe dismissed the confession too lightly because he'd fudged up the details. Maybe they'd misjudged his motive too. Was his confession, that he counted on having disbelieved, a cover for his own guilt rather than his suspicion of Fiona's?

Mitchell pulled down the car's visor against the bright June sun and put his foot down, unaware that George Gregson was busy preparing his library for a staff meeting.

Adrian Naylor drummed his fingers on the library table. This wasn't a vital meeting, it was just another opportunity for the Great George Gregson to sound off at his staff. He thought because he'd nothing better to do than listen to the sound of his own voice that no one else had. What if Fi was waiting for him, shut out, at his front door?

He could see her there, consumed with terror, clutching at her suitcase handle and trying not to scream. He half rose to excuse himself and rush off to deal with this vivid imaginary scene but was restrained by the other half of his mind that showed him an alternative picture. Fi was looking round her own flat with satisfaction, ringing the hospital to say that her condition was much improved and could she begin her duties again very soon? He felt consumed with guilt for hoping the first vision was the more accurate one.

Gregson was irate. He had received three letters of complaint because Detective Sergeant Hunter had been spying on his pupils at their rehearsal. 'One was from Derek Saxby, of course.' The staff all groaned softly. 'But another was from Asif Malik who's usually a very reasonable sort of man, much less trouble to us than his daughter. He says he has no objection at all to Wendy being properly interviewed but he doesn't like this underhand way of gaining the children's confidence. I must say I have some sympathy with him.

'The third one is from Mr Cunningham and is as abusive as you might imagine. Why he imputes blame to us for police activity I fail to understand and I shall not quote him. I won't incense you, or give him the satisfaction of having his opinions generally listened to.'

Abusive or not, Naylor concluded, he had been more fluent than Gregson himself and was therefore to be deprived of his moment of glory.

He tried to unclench his jaw and relax a little. If he could break down all his worries into separate items he could perhaps deal with some of them. What had Detective Constable Mitchell been saying to Mrs T? The call she'd mentioned had puzzled her and upset him with its mention of his excuse for being late at the church. It had to be Fi who had told them that. Did she suspect him—and did the police?

Gregson was explaining the arrangements he'd made for a supply teacher. Why had his share of cover for Julia's absence had to be that dreadful third-form lot? He answered his own question. Kit Travers had volunteered herself for the easy-to-manage exam forms who worked because it suited them to.

He looked up, startled, at the sound of his own name. No worry. It was just a perfunctory mention in a list of those whose efforts to keep the play rolling were receiving the expected public acknowledgement. 'The parents, too, are supporting our plans to press on.' His satisfaction at this state of affairs led Gregson into indiscretion. 'I'm quite sure that no business connected with school is relevant to police enquiries. They need to look into the young woman's private life.'

This was indignantly challenged. 'I don't know quite what you mean by that!' Naylor smiled. Gregson had obviously forgotten that Julia was Kit Travers' relation. He hastened to soothe her.

'I didn't mean to suggest the least impropriety—just a contact she may have had, or someone she may have inadvertently annoyed.'

Kit Travers subsided, still looking thunderous. Why was Mrs T so het up? Naylor wondered. He hadn't had the impression that she and her cousin were the best of friends, in spite of her recommendation that Julia should fill their temporary gap.

Eventually the meeting ground to a halt. Even Gregson began to want his tea more than further exercise of his power complex. Naylor stretched his legs into the space left as Phil Brooke moved to the window. 'Hello, the fuzz is here again.'

Blind panic filled Naylor. He could hardly get up from his chair. Was this how Fi felt all the time? He'd vowed he'd finished with all that, but suddenly he could not bring himself to walk past Mitchell's car to his own at the gate without just one more injection. Thank the Lord it was Michael's supplies Hunter had found and not his own.

When he emerged from the cloakroom some ten minutes later, he noticed with a sinking heart that many of his colleagues' cars had gone but that Mitchell's was still parked. He went outside and walked rapidly to his vehicle, aware of the sound of Mitchell's feet behind him, then his shadow.

Mitchell noted the bright eyes, dilated pupils and the forefinger tapping on the metal door. He was philosophical. Naylor hardly talked a great deal of sense when he wasn't high. He would hope that today's nervous babble would be even less discreet than usual.

When his questions were finished and he had let Naylor go, Mitchell was still in two minds. Why should he have gone to Julia's house just before two on Sunday to try to beg Fiona off the charity walk? Why couldn't they just not turn up? Or why could the matter not be discussed when he and Julia met at school as, unless he had killed her, he would have expected them to do?

Mitchell found Naylor's explanation of his actions after the rehearsal quite credible in the light of the rest of his conduct, though when it was repeated to Petty, it would sound ludicrous. His face split into a grin as he imagined giving his report. 'Tell me again, Mitchell. He waited till everyone had gone, then put on his favourite velvet costume, meant for a character called Philostrate?'

'Yes, sir.'

'And left his clothes backstage whilst he went up the back stairs to look at himself in the needlework room mirror?' In Mitchell's imagination, Petty's voice rose in incredulity. 'Go on, man!'

'Sir, when he was ready to change back, the caretaker was replacing a lock on an outside door at the bottom of the stairs. He dared not show himself in pale blue velvet—the caretaker has never liked him anyway and would be certain to share the joke with the whole school. He had to wait up there an hour and a half before the man went away.'

Out of his presence, Mitchell could theorize about Naylor's duplicity, pretence of fecklessness and inability to cope. With the man in front of him his inadequacy was unequivocal. Killing, Mitchell thought, was too decisive an action for Naylor to achieve.

Chapter 17

Hunter had carried out to the best of his ability the instructions he had received from his superintendent. He intended to finish his day's work by following up a hunch of his own. Apart from explaining her presence at Laura Saxby's house yesterday, he was sure there was more that Helen Rowe could tell him about the people involved in this case.

He drew up at the front gate in Compton Road, which he had to open carefully to avoid damage to the magnificent dark red blooms of the rhododendron bush that grew beside it. He regarded the shrub thoughtfully. Its opulence was unfitting to English moderation in general and to the low-key, under-stated scuffed delicacy of the vegetation in this part of Yorkshire in particular. It had its own attraction, of course. He shook back his hair, decided his hangover had completely disappeared and knocked at the door.

Helen invited him in and explained that her mother was helping at the old people's day centre and her father was out, summoned by Derek Saxby for a purpose unspecified.

Hunter congratulated himself on his foresight in having brought along a WPC and signalled back to his car for her to follow him in. He would have liked a confidential chat to Helen on her own, with her mother a discreet presence out in the kitchen. He hoped that Janet Merry would either establish a rapport with the girl or withdraw herself from the proceedings.

Helen led them both to the dining room, her skirt swinging round her bustling hips. It had fussy rows of a little black motif on an aquamarine ground and made Hunter think of tadpoles doing synchronized swimming. Dress sense was one aspect of Helen's mind that was not developed in advance of her years.

Feeling that it was a shabby way to treat such a straightforward girl, he nevertheless began the interview by asking her how she had enjoyed her day in Manchester. She replied, carefully, that there had certainly been plenty of food for thought.

'Tell me about it.'

Helen gave herself time by tucking both legs underneath her and arranging her skirt in neat folds. 'There was a lecture to begin with about the balance between the playwright's input and the actors'—you know, freedom of interpretation. Then everybody was put in a group to prepare a scene from *Hobson's Choice*. We'd all been asked to read it beforehand. Do you know it?'

Hunter nodded. 'I saw it in Leeds years ago and it's been on television too. Not highbrow but good theatre. Which bit did you do?'

'Where Maggie's getting her father to pay compensation for damaging the corn sacks so that she can use the money for her sister's marriage settlement.'

'You'd make a good Maggie. Is that the part you were given?' Helen flushed scarlet and Hunter could not persist. She had answered his previous questions truthfully with information she had obtained from Emma and Wendy, but to insist on an answer to this was to force her to lie.

'You weren't there, were you, Helen?'

'So you did see me.' She looked relieved that the teasing was over and the direct attack about to begin.

Hunter nodded. 'Why? I'd have thought you'd have been keen—'

'I can't tell you!'

'I have to know. If not from you then from someone else.'

She was defiant now. 'Aunt Laura won't tell you.'

'Then I shall have to try your parents and the other two girls.'

There was a silence but it was not sullen. He watched her, wondering wildly how to protect whatever secret she was keeping. It was time to change tack. 'How many people was Michael supplying with amphetamines, Helen?' She froze. 'Come on, we've a pretty good idea and what we don't know yet we shall find out from someone. The sooner some of them get the help they need, the better.'

This had been the right line. She was softening. 'What about you?'

'I've never touched it.' He believed her. 'Dan's on it for sure, though he doesn't know I know about it. Michael made sure I did. He gets as many kicks out of knowing

311

how I feel about it as he does out of the power he has to make sure Dan keeps winning. Dan would never have done it if he hadn't been out of his mind about his mother, but it's no excuse, is it? I'd still like to help him but it's finished us as a couple.

'Emma was on it for a while. She's keen on sport and her father saw her as a female counterpart of Dan. She won a few things and her parents were full of it but she came off the stuff when she got pregnant.'

'What?'

She raised her shoulders then dropped them hopelessly. 'I might as well tell you. You're going to get there in the end.'

Light was beginning to dawn on Hunter. 'This is to do with yesterday?' She encouraged him with a nod. 'You didn't go to Manchester because Emma was having a bad morning. You both took refuge at her Aunt Laura's house.'

She shook her head. 'Well, we did but it was different. We found out Wendy was going on this course. Dr Travers managed to get Emma's appointment fixed for the same day. Aunt Laura knew all about it. She took Wendy to Manchester, then took Emma and me to the hospital. I stayed

312

with Emma and then we went home together and I did some school work. We stayed at Aunt Laura's till she'd been back to fetch Wendy and then she took all of us home.'

Hunter frowned. 'But that's ridiculous. What excuse is she going to make for the next appointment? And however long does she think it will stay a secret?' He stopped at Helen's impatient exclamation.

'It's gone now!'

'You mean Emma had an abortion yesterday?'

Helen nodded. 'I don't think I could do it myself, but then, I haven't been in her position and I haven't got her parents—and, most important, I didn't have Michael's baby inside me. It might have turned out as nasty as its father and he wouldn't have helped her.'

Both officers remained still and quiet, watching Helen pick at a loose thread in her skirt, but when she continued to speak there was not much more to tell. 'Emma went out with Michael because her father told her not to. She'd decided she'd never have any life until she'd learned to stand up to him—but she's still afraid of him really. I'm so sorry for her and so sorry

313

about Dan.' Suddenly, Helen was in floods of tears and Janet Merry, hitherto silent, proved her worth.

Home from his day's interviewing, Browne felt refreshed by the change of activity and ready to go back to his investigation with renewed interest. He'd leave Petty in charge of his men for another half hour though, whilst he went home to change and remind himself that he had a wife.

A little disappointed to find Hannah ironing rather than minding Declan, he still offered to prepare a snack meal after he'd put on something comfortable. He threw off his suit with relief, remembered to hang it neatly, showered and put on flannels and a sweatshirt.

He looked out of the window as he did up buttons and brushed his hair. The gracious houses just beyond the end of the garden were on a private road, half hidden by trees. He noted that the green mist on their branches, which, last time he had had a minute to notice, had been just forming into separate leaves, had now solidified into balls of dark green foliage.

He was irritated by it. Whilst this case had been going on, he'd been hurried into summer before he was ready for it.

Beyond the private road, at the foot of the slope on the other side of the valley, was a hideous row of 'town houses', 'detached' because you could just about slide a piece of paper between them. There had been fresh moans from Hannah when a second row further defaced the hillside, but, for Browne, once the first lot were there its character had already changed.

Not that he minded the change, but the hillside now had another purpose for him. He no longer used it to loosen himself from hassles but looked to it for stimulation. The busy little social climbers living there repaid his observation of them by amusing him and occasionally teaching him new lessons about the nature of the human race—or at least the section of it that peopled that particular hill.

He couldn't work out why the houses were so offensive to him when he could take mill chimneys cheerfully in his stride. Perhaps the chimneys' patina of dirt helped them blend in with the rest. Or, maybe, he'd reached an age when he could only accept what was familiar and automatically rejected any innovation. No, he finally decided. It was because there was no pretence about a mill chimney.

A telegraph pole at the bottom of his own road supported wires stretching in all directions to the surrounding houses. It looked like a dowdy maypole, its ribbons drab and thin but ready for the dance to begin.

Dusk was deepening and the lights were appearing. He loved watching them, street lamps and windows and headlights from the traffic on the M62 on the horizon. Later tonight, when he sat up in bed, he would watch them with their promise that life would continue busily whilst he rested before joining in again. What he felt like doing this evening was having one of his sessions with Jerry, closeted in his tiny study, making inroads into his supply of home brew and taking the case to pieces, but Hannah had put paid to that plan.

She had stacked his chair and his lamp and his bookcase on to his desk and covered the whole with a dust sheet. Then she had taken down the curtains and torn all the paper off the walls. And finally she had told him that if he wanted to use the place again, he'd better get on with decorating it. Then she would put everything back.

Like a Mancunian woman she had set up the sewing machine in the sitting room and covered the rest of the furniture with the fabric for his new curtains, which in future would annoy him instead of Jerry because there would be no chinks in the middle.

Oh well, it would have to be the pub again, but it wouldn't be the same. He would have to wear decent shoes instead of tatty slippers, and who could think a case through properly wearing shoes? He clattered downstairs and began to bang about the kitchen as Hannah attacked the last shirt with the iron and wondered what on earth had irritated him now.

Hunter, too, was contemplating the dusk in melancholy mood. He felt sad for Helen, sad for Emma and her dead baby, sad for Daniel. Schooldays were supposed to be your happiest and he had enjoyed his own, but these children must have felt sorely burdened as they trotted along to their prestigious school. Everyone in Cloughton thought that, at that one if no other, innocent youth was being prepared for a full and useful life.

Of course, pupils these days were not

only not innocent, they were not young. They were old enough, as Emma and Michael had proved, to reproduce. When his own parents were Cunningham's age they had been in work for three years and on the brink of marriage.

Was that why it had all gone wrong? Should youngsters be allowed to learn about life by living it rather than getting everything out of books. What were you supposed to do with your spirit of adventure when all that was required of you to be approved was to express yourself in an essay or answer lists of questions, especially if you had to give an account of yourself afterwards if one of your classmates had scored more points than you?

He could hear the strains of Tim's oboe as the lad practised upstairs. He asked himself whether his son was playing because he enjoyed it or because he himself had always wanted to own and play an instrument. Annette was busy in the kitchen attending to his cricket gear. That at least, Hunter was sure, Tim took part in for his own pleasure.

He was a pleasant lad, well mannered, bright enough but no high flier. He wouldn't be going off to university like Alex and Virginia Browne. Fliss too, though good at art and interested in ballet, was no scholar. Her school exercises were beautifully neat and tidy but showed little academic promise. He thought he and Annette accepted them both just as they were but, all the same, he'd have a word with Tim about the oboe.

Meanwhile, he looked for something to pull him out of his disillusion and wandered over to his collection of CDs. Elisabeth Schwarzkopf could sing to him his beloved Four Last Songs. Richard Strauss could always do the trick. But he didn't. Even as the violin soared in accompaniment to the third song, his favourite, bits and pieces of the case continued to float about in his mind... You'd make a good Maggie...Dan's on it for sure...just remind you that my housekeeping is not of a standard...an exemplary, Mass-every-Sunday, no-meat-on-Friday member of Sacred Heart...Julia would hardly have filed it under his initials if she'd wanted to ring them... Oh my God! He leapt for the phone.

Browne picked it up at the first ring. 'Hello, Jerry. I was just about to ring you. It's time we had a session but I've been turfed out of my own den. Do you fancy the Shears? It's about halfway between us—or shall we drive out to the Tiller—'

Hunter cut in, 'I wouldn't mind a quick one but I think we've got more work to do.'

'What, tonight?'

'I think so. It had better be the Shears. It's handier.'

On the grounds that the seriousness of their talk had ruined the taste of the first pint they stretched a point and had another as they made their plans. 'We'll stick to the people we're already familiar with so that means Laura Saxby for you and Travers for me. See you back here when we've heard what they have to say.'

Left alone outside the Superintendent's office, Dean soon abandoned his wait. The only useful information he had gained from carrying out Petty's instructions he had just handed over to Mitchell. If Benny could take off and find himself something useful to do to finish the afternoon, then so could he. The CI wasn't an unreasonable chap. He was always slapping down Benny's attempts to run the show but it was obvious why he had to do that. It was the price Benny had to pay for marrying Virginia. Not that she wasn't worth it, although she certainly wasn't his cup of tea—too bossy by half—but she suited Benny. He evidently liked a drop of his own medicine. Now, what should he do?

It was beginning to seem to Dean that Neil Stevens was a suspect they had neglected. They had considered his activities only in terms of their being an alibi for Daniel. He would have had oceans of time to commit the murder himself, with his wife safely away at the hospice and Daniel at his play rehearsal. Hadn't there been a message from him to Julia on Hilary Deakin's answering machine? Presumably he'd explained what it was about to Browne—Dean cursed himself for not having read all the case notes carefully enough—but whatever excuse he made he could really have made an arrangement to meet Julia on her way to the Sunday afternoon rehearsal. He'd been free to get up to anything he liked.

And he'd been handy on the canal path at the right time, arriving well before Jack Nicholls and playing the conscientious father. 'Dan's bound to be along well before any of the others. I don't want my lad to put anyone to any extra trouble. Don't worry, I'll be early.' They had considered whether a parent of a pupil on drugs might have killed to preserve a child's reputation. It would be doubly important to Neil Stevens that there should be no unpleasant scandal about his son just now. It would be imperative to him that his wife should die believing that her pride in her son was justified.

Whilst his brain had been busy his feet had carried him to his car. As he climbed in he half hoped he was wrong. He would hate to be the one who added to the woman's distress by revealing her husband as a killer. He shook his head and turned the ignition key. He was getting soft! Three minutes into his journey, Dean saw his quarry on the opposite side of the road. He flashed the Volvo, which returned his signal as Stevens recognized Dean's vehicle but did not stop. He sighed. Might as well continue to the house. He might have another session with Daniel if he was in and he might find out where Neil Stevens was bound.

Against his better judgement, Stevens had obeyed a summons by telephone from

Saxby. Several other cars were parked across the front of the house. He tucked the Volvo in neatly beside Vernon Rowe's Escort and examined the rest, trying to work out who else had been considered sufficiently important to give voice to his opinions in Saxby's drawing room. Clare Saxby answered his ring and ushered him in to join the company. Her husband was in mid-bluster on the subject of unmannerly policemen who asked irrelevant questions of innocent citizens. He rose to shake hands with Stevens and glanced out of the window. What he saw gave rise to an irritated exclamation. 'I asked Brenda Malik to come to but it's that black beggar who's rolled up. I suppose you'd better let him in.' Clare had already departed to do so. Saxby fussed in the corner whilst they waited for Malik to come in, pouring more sherry and making sure, Stevens noted, that the 'black beggar' was given short measure. Eventually they were settled and Saxby resumed his harangue. 'I'm sure we all wish the bloody woman had never been taken on but since things are as they are, how are we to protect our young folk?'

Vernon Rowe looked puzzled. 'Protect them? From what? Do you think whoever

323

attacked Miss Feather might plan an assault on one of them?'

Saxby looked startled. 'There's that too, of course, but I meant from the police. Don't you think we should all insist on being present when our children are being interviewed? That gangly sergeant made out that in police terms Emma and all the others are not minors, but in effect they are. The only world they know is school. They aren't up to the tricks of the nasty world and they shouldn't be at the mercy of men who are paid to nail a crime wherever it will stick as quickly as possible.'

Rowe was not impressed. 'From some of the things Helen's said in the last couple of weeks, Holmbrooke could teach the nasty world a trick or two.'

'But for the police's own benefit, surely our children will speak more freely if we're there to support them.'

Looking round the room, Stevens could see that he was not alone in doubting this assertion. Only Cunningham seemed to support Saxby's opinions. 'Those coppers certainly want watching. They took my place apart for no reason—though I must admit they didn't leave any mess. They'd have heard from me about it if they had. And Michael's more than a match for any copper. If Paul isn't, now's the time for him to learn.'

Malik spoke up. 'I cannot think who would want to kill a perfectly respectable girl. She attended a church. She teaches in school. You do not expect a teacher to be killed with a knife—'

'It's not so long since,' Saxby interrupted, 'that the paper was full of a story of a boy knifing one of his masters as he went out to his car. He wasn't given much of a punishment as far as I can remember. No discipline these days.'

Stevens wondered which side Saxby was arguing for. Vernon Rowe spoke for him, getting to his feet. 'The police have been perfectly civil to my family and Miss Feather has done a great deal for Helen—not just with the play. She's enthused her over her set texts too. I don't think this meeting's getting anywhere.'

Stevens added his support. 'There's nothing we can do. The police haven't exceeded their powers and, personally, there's nothing I want to do except give all possible assistance to them in getting the whole matter cleared up.' Feeling he sounded rather pompous, he followed Rowe out, avoiding Saxby's glare. He saw that another car had joined those parked outside and when the driver's door opened he recognized DC Dean.

Dean was shocked at the change in the man since their last meeting. It was in the droop of his mouth and his shoulders and it changed his whole aspect. He asked Stevens to remind him of the details of the message he left on Hilary Deakin's answering machine. The man gave him a sardonic glance and obliged. 'I needed transport for Daniel to a training session in Leeds. Dan's learning to drive. He'll be able to take himself soon. I could have taken him myself but I'm spending all the time I can with Janet and Julia said she'd do anything at all to help. She rang me back and said she'd take him and another Holmbrooke boy.'

'When?'

'Last Friday—a week ago today when she rang and Saturday afternoon when she took them. Dan didn't seem very grateful and I thought then that he didn't want to be beholden to her, that he thought he ought to have got a bus or a train.'

'Then?'

Stevens shook his head, sadly. 'I gather you know all about it, Constable Dean.' He looked round, embarrassed, as the rest of Saxby's visitors came down the front steps. Dean opened his passenger door. 'Let's go somewhere more private.'

Stevens nodded. 'Not the station,' he pleaded, 'and not my place. Dan will think you've come to run him in. Let's walk in the park. I can explain better if we're not sitting looking at one another.'

Dean calculated the risk in letting Stevens drive his own car, then decided to take it. He drove there, keeping an eye on his rear-view mirror, and waited till Stevens had parked beside him. They walked together down the main path, both of them unaware of the glory of rhododendrons that burned on either side of them in the late evening sun. Stevens was the first to break the silence. 'I suppose you've known all along that Dan was cheating. I've only known since last Wednesday. He came home from his play practice and told me all about it. He asked me to help him, both to get off the stuff and to face up to confessing that he'd used it.'

'And since then you've been wondering whether it was Dan who tried to shut Miss Feather up about it, especially after a lecture on Saturday that lasted all the way to Leeds and back.'

Suddenly Stevens was down on the path. Dean, with accusations of police brutality seriously on his mind, felt for a pulse in his neck. It was there, thank goodness, and strengthening. He helped his suspect on to an ornamental bench and offered to call an ambulance. Stevens shook his head. 'No, but we'll sit for a bit. That wasn't what I was wondering. It hadn't occurred to me. I was having difficulty in believing even what he told me. Are you telling me that's what the police believe?'

'Not necessarily.' Dean waited as his patient's breath still came unevenly. He was convinced that the man's shock was genuine and the suspicions that had instigated this interview had dissipated. He took the plunge. 'Personally, I'm sure not. I haven't seen much of your lad but in this job you have to sum folk up quickly. I don't believe he's really enjoyed his apparent successes and it must have taken a degree of integrity and a lot of courage to come clean with you.'

'I've got to rethink the lad completely.'

'I don't think so. Your wife's illness has made things very difficult for both of you. He'll learn from this, to understand how other people can go off the rails and that it's possible to climb back. He's begun that already.'

Dean wondered at himself. He sounded like old man Browne—possibly he even felt like him. Not more than a few months since he had wanted undeniable proof before he believed a suspect innocent.

'Does his mother have to find out?'

Dean shrugged. 'Considering Dan's family circumstances and his present attitude, I don't think he's likely to be prosecuted—but you must bear in mind that Michael will be and we can't gag him. How clean you come in sporting circles is none of our business.'

When Stevens left him to drive home he rang the station and thankfully learned that neither Browne nor Petty was there to report to. He wondered whether to slake the dust of the evening at the Shears. He'd made a loose arrangement that he might see Benny there to compare notes on their individual evenings. On the other hand, he'd half promised Metcalfe he'd try a jog round his beginners' course if he got a chance over the weekend—and it wasn't likely to be a quiet one.

He made history half an hour later. Clutching a bag containing a vest, shorts and his Reebok trainers, he walked in the direction of a prefabricated shack on the edge of a field, deliberately passing by the hostelry in which his three colleagues were preparing to wind up the case.

The Shears' landlord, who had overheard Browne's last remark before he left, decided that, whoever those people were that it had been so urgent to consult, they had said very little, since his two customers were back at their table in half an hour. The dark man and the fair drank iced tonic water and fresh orange juice respectively and talked solemnly but Laura Saxby and Travers had obviously come up with the goods. The landlord detected a quiet satisfaction in their demeanour.

They were joined after a few minutes by a fatter, younger, bullet-headed man who seemed to have come in for a quick pint and met them by chance. The landlord gathered that, since the newcomer hadn't time before last orders to drink himself over the limit, he had earned his welcome with an offer to drive the other two home. At any rate, the soft drinks were abandoned in favour of bitter and draught cider.

'That horse is terminal,' the young man remarked as he handed over the half pint. It was evidently a running joke and the tall man smiled as he surveyed the murky contents of his glass. The landlord returned to his clearing up as his three customers conferred.

'Are we doing the pick up tonight?'

Browne looked at his watch. 'I think not. If we're right, and I'm sure we are, it's not as though anyone else is in danger.'

'It's the first time,' Hunter remarked, 'that we've had the ghost of a serious motive.' They all nodded.

'Quarter past eight in the morning,' Browne decided. 'They'll probably all be at home. You can go, Benny. My car will still be here and you'll be a new face to them. Let's hope Jennie makes it in the morning. We could do with her on hand.'

Chapter 18

Refreshed by twelve hours' sleep and sustained by her new and peculiar breakfast menu, Jennie Taylor turned up on Saturday morning ready to work doubly hard to atone for her evening's default. She felt faintly resentful that during her absence the case seemed to have broken and faintly pleased that a deduction of Hunter's rather than a suggestion of Mitchell's had brought it about for a change.

She was pleased to find Browne had decreed that she should conduct the interview with the accused.

As she went into the interview room, she felt an urge to apologize. It appeared not to have been cleaned for some time. She was aware of the girl's distaste for her surroundings and felt repelled by them herself. A full ash tray, a dried up sticky pool of spilt liquid and a dead wasp on the surface of the table was the only relief when she averted her gaze from the peeling walls and uncurtained window through which the sunlight condemned the squalor.

Browne remained standing in the doorway as Jennie approached one of the plastic stacking chairs and sternly regarded the occupant of the other across the table. 'All right, Emma, let's have no more lies and denials. Tell us what happened.' The girl sat, silent and sullen, her head bent as though her twisting fingers were the only objects in the room on which she could bear to rest her eyes.

'We know where Miss Feather's car was hidden between ten minutes to two and late on Sunday evening.' The sullen silence continued. 'Well, you know where it was, of course, but perhaps you'd like to know how we found out. Your Aunt Laura just happened to remark to Sergeant Hunter last night that she popped round to your house on Sunday afternoon. Your parents had offered her some flowers. She chose to come and pick them when she knew you would be rehearsing so that you wouldn't think she was trying to spy on you.

'She passed the garage on the way to the shed to look for garden scissors and some string and she happened to notice a red Fiat in the garage. She wondered which friend you had staying with you but she didn't ask because she'd promised you a weekend's privacy.'

When there was still no response, Jennie tried a different approach. 'I'm pregnant too. My baby's due in December.' Emma remained silent but transferred her gaze from her own hands to Jennie's. 'Yes, all right, I love the father, I've got a husband and it's all very pleasant for me. Tell me how it was for you.'

Emma's voice was low, and Jennie casually pushed the microphone nearer to her. 'I stopped taking the drugs when I realized I might be pregnant. I stopped doing my running as well although Dr Travers told me later I needn't have done that. When I'd stopped hoping I might be mistaken, I did a home test. It was positive.' Tears rolled down her cheeks but her voice remained controlled. 'I thought at first that I could marry Michael, have the baby and get away from home.'

Jennie produced a packet of tissues from her handbag and asked, 'How did Miss Feather find out about it?'

Emma shrugged. 'I was ill in her registration period several mornings running. I told her it was a nervous problem—even

Mrs T believed that. She knows what my father is like—but Miss Feather went on and on at me. When you're concentrating hard on not throwing up, you haven't got your wits about you.' She helped herself to another tissue. 'She said she'd help me to tell my parents and I got hysterical and said they must never know.'

'She said, "You surely don't mean..." I hadn't been able to put it into words myself until then but, when she couldn't say it, I felt suddenly sure of myself. I said, "Yes, an abortion." Then she really got started.'

'So, when she offered to pick you up and talk to you on the way to school you really knew what it was about?'

She nodded, bit her lip, recommenced the finger twisting. 'I got desperate. She said if she couldn't convince me herself she'd have to get my father on her side. She said she couldn't let me commit murder without making every possible effort to stop me. When I said I'd make some coffee, she thought I was coming round. She pushed me a bit further, told me to go in the kitchen by myself and really think about it. There was nothing to think about and I told her so.' For the first time the voice rose and broke. 'She called me a murderess and now I am!'

Jennie waited quietly for her to regain sufficient composure to go on. 'I still had the pills and the syringes. I crept upstairs to get them and mixed the powder with some lemon juice out of the fridge. I had a quick swig of my father's whisky before the injection, then, as soon as I felt the flash, crept back in.'

Jennie and Browne exchanged glances. So, the girl had actually meant to kill—or at least to threaten. She had prepared herself for it as best she could.

'She didn't hear me, never turned round. I couldn't believe I'd done it. She didn't seem any different except that she wasn't talking. Then I knew she must be dead or she'd never have stopped talking, talking, talking...' She began to cry out loud, letting the tears fall unchecked, howling like a hurt toddler. Jennie watched her dispassionately until she quietened, then handed her another tissue. Emma took it, mopped her face cursorily and asked for a glass of water.

When it was brought she drank in silence, handed the empty glass over and remarked, conversationally, 'I pulled her

336

woollen hat completely over her head, covering her face as well. I couldn't stand her looking at me.'

Browne, standing unobtrusively by the door, kicked himself mentally. He could guess the rest. He had considered the body having fallen from the Rocks but could not understand how it could have left Julia's face unmarked. Even the smears of make-up inside the hat had not told him. He must have been half asleep.

'How did you manage to get through the rehearsal?' Jennie was asking.

Emma almost smiled. 'It was easy because I wasn't being me for most of the afternoon—and I was still high, of course, for a while. I backed the Fiat into the garage and shut the doors. Then I drew the curtains in the dining room and went down to the gate to look for whoever was going to pick me up. I nearly passed out afterwards, though. It was in Michael's car and Helen helped me.'

'How much does Helen know?'

'Only about the baby.'

'And the drugs?'

Emma nodded. 'When it got dark, I fetched the wheelbarrow out of the shed. I was hoping I might lose the baby while I was humping the body into it but I didn't. That's life, isn't it? Miscarriages only happen to people who really want their babies, don't they? Anyway, I just wheeled the barrow to the bottom of the garden and along the edge of the Rocks a fair way, tipped it over, then wheeled it back home. I was on pins when Mother was complaining in front of Sergeant Hunter about her best sharp vegetable knife that I'd chipped the end off, but he didn't catch on, thank goodness.' Browne supposed he couldn't blame Hunter. The PM report hadn't arrived then to tell them the small chip of metal had been found in the wound.

'And the car?'

'I put my duffle on with the hood up, drove it to the car park of the pub where Michael said he took Miss Feather, then walked home and rang Aunt Laura to fetch me.' Most of the information had come out tonelessly, in jerky phrases, but now Emma was speaking smoothly, just making conversation, her hands relaxed.

'Feel better for talking about it?'

She nodded. 'Can I go all through the trial like this, with them out of the way?'

She jerked her head towards the reception area to which her parents with their threats and objections had been banished.

'Could you do that to them?'

'Why not? It's nothing compared with what they've done to me. Whatever sort of prison you send me to, it's going to be perfect freedom compared to living with them.'

Epilogue

When her labour pains were twenty minutes apart, Jennie Taylor had driven herself to the maternity hospital. Being conducted, to give birth to her first child, by an anxiously attentive husband was not to be counted on by a police wife. Paul was attending an accident on the M62 and just at that moment she hadn't wanted to hear about it.

She had proceeded carefully over a couple of inches of snow along their own street and been thankful to find the gritters had been in action over the rest of her route. Things had progressed quickly and her stay in the labour ward had been brief. Now she found herself in the delivery room, wheeled there by an orderly dressed in a dark green smock.

She surveyed the table on to which she was about to be transferred and the complicated harness contraption suspended above it. It seemed that the procedure for the delivery of a baby was almost as absurd as the procedure for its conception—but with less choice for the main participant.

She looked down at the strange garment she had been required to wear on her upper half, then tried to work out what ungainly position she would have to adopt in the harness. Finally, she imagined the undignified noises that would probably accompany her efforts to part company for the first time with her infant. Thank goodness, at least, that no one she knew would see her and that she was unlikely to meet again, at any rate till next time, any of the people who attended her.

A girl in a white gown came in. Her golden brown corkscrew curls were pulled back severely under a functional white cap. She had a short, turned-up nose and hazel eyes with incredibly long lashes, and a promise of attractive curves beneath the shapeless cotton wrap. This was not the midwife Jennie had met and expected.

She tried to sound pleased to see her. 'Hello, Fiona.'

'Mrs Unwin's off with flu.' Fiona's delight was unfeigned. 'I was in at the beginning with this baby—saved it from malnutrition. I'm glad to be seeing it through to the end.'

Another contraction interrupted the polite conversation. Fiona's ministrations were competent and impersonal and Jennie found they could both ignore her grunts.

At rest again, she was amused when Fiona asked, 'Do you mind if I ask you some questions?'

'That puts the boot on the other leg. Go on, then.'

'They're about the case. Once I'd got away from Adrian I kept away. I read about the outcome in the paper, of course, but I've often wondered how all the others were getting on.'

'I'll tell you what I can. It's six months ago now though. We've been busy on other cases and I've been out of things myself for some weeks. Mrs Stevens died before all the ends of the affair were tied up. Daniel dropped his sporting activities. He gave back all his trophies and settled down to his A-levels. I know about him because when he was eighteen he joined the Specials. He's thinking about applying to join the force.' She bit her lip and began her rhythmic breathing again.

Fiona was startled. 'That was quick. You're well dilated. It shouldn't be much longer. All right now?'

Jennie nodded.

'What about Adrian?'

Jennie shook her head. 'As far as I know, same place, same job, same complaints...' She broke off as, for the first time in very many, Lucy-Jane Taylor claimed her mother's exclusive attention and put a stop to her conversation.

Emma Saxby was not finding her incarceration any more unpleasant than she had anticipated. She had missed Helen and Dan and the rest of her friends at first, but here she had met other interesting people and had seen that many of their problems had less chance of being resolved than her own.

She had been chary in the beginning about the countless and inevitable interviews with psychiatrists and social workers, but she found to her surprise that they had actually wanted to listen to her. They had introduced her to the heady experience of searching her own mind and making her own decisions. She had been particularly amused when she had been offered counselling to help her come to terms with her parents' decision to stop seeing her. She had been dreading their visits and found the existing arrangements totally satisfactory.

She was only sorry that her mother, doubtless nudged and harried by Aunt Laura, had gone back on her decision so far as to write to her. Emma was determined not to answer the letter, but she glanced at it again, the phrases, after only a first reading, coming familiarly back to her. Mother could still pack a punch or two on paper when she was at one removed from her enemy.

'Neither Father nor I have been very well recently, which, in the circumstances, is hardly surprising. Father has been promising to write. I suppose he actually might one day when he has nothing better to do. Meanwhile, I suppose... We shall just about have patched up the tattered remnants of our lives when you'll be out again. I'm sure it's going to take as long as that... Your notoriety hasn't done your father's business any good... It will be better for everyone if you make a fresh start somewhere else.

'Father says we should have been stricter with you and, for once, I think he's right...I've had to leave the Inner Wheel. I wasn't going to give them the chance to

345

snub me, though I'm sure what's happened is no fault of mine. Laura tells me she writes to you. I'm sure you don't deserve it, but then, if she hadn't encouraged you...'

Emma folded the sheets and put them back into the envelope before reaching for her Biology text book. Switching to science A-levels had been a good idea. A career in saving lives would help as well as anything to atone for the two she had destroyed. But, first, she had something else to destroy. She took the two folded sheets of paper back out of their envelope and tugged at them.

When nothing happened, she smiled to herself. Who did her mother think there was here who would be impressed by paper of that quality? She unfolded the sheets again and took them singly, tearing them into shreds and scattering them over the floor.

This Large Print Book for the Partially sighted, who cannot read normal print, is published under the auspices of

THE ULVERSCROFT FOUNDATION

THE ULVERSCROFT FOUNDATION

. . . we hope that you have enjoyed this Large Print Book. Please think for a moment about those people who have worse eyesight problems than you . . . and are unable to even read or enjoy Large Print, without great difficulty.

You can help them by sending a donation, large or small to:

**The Ulverscroft Foundation,
1, The Green, Bradgate Road,
Anstey, Leicestershire, LE7 7FU,
England.**

or request a copy of our brochure for more details.

The Foundation will use all your help to assist those people who are handicapped by various sight problems and need special attention.

Thank you very much for your help.

Other MAGNA Mystery Titles In Large Print

WILLIAM HAGGARD
The Vendettists

C. F. ROE
Death By Fire

MARJORIE ECCLES
Cast A Cold Eye

KEITH MILES
Bullet Hole

PAULINE G. WINSLOW
A Cry In The City

DEAN KOONTZ
Watchers

KEN McCLURE
Pestilence